**"But the colonel was acting
on his own initiative, wasn't he, sir?"**

Conway nodded. "He was—but the colonel has friends in high places. At the same time, headquarters has had enough of his nonsense." Conway's face was hard as he said, "Matt, your assignment is Fort Stambaugh."

"And the orders, sir?" Matt Kincaid asked.

"You are to stop Colonel Blue..."

EASY COMPANY

EASY COMPANY

AND THE WHISKEY TRAIN

JOHN WESLEY HOWARD

A JOVE BOOK

EASY COMPANY AND THE WHISKEY TRAIN

A Jove Book/published by arrangement with
the author

PRINTING HISTORY
Jove edition/August 1983

ISBN: 0-515-06363-0

Jove books are published by The Berkley Publishing Group,
200 Madison Avenue, New York, N.Y. 10016. The words
"A JOVE BOOK" and the "J" with sunburst are trademarks
belonging to Jove Publications, Inc.

PRINTED IN THE UNITED STATES OF AMERICA

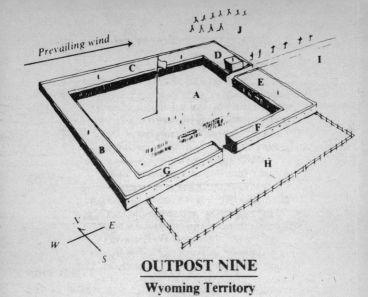

OUTPOST NINE

Wyoming Territory

KEY

A. Parade and flagstaff

B. Officers' quarters ("officers' country")

C. Enlisted men's quarters: barracks, day room, and mess

D. Kitchen, quartermaster supplies, ordnance shop, guardhouse

E. Suttler's store and other shops, tack room, and smithy

F. Stables

G. Quarters for dependents and guests; communal kitchen

H. Paddock

I. Road and telegraph line to regimental headquarters

J. Indian camp occupied by transient "friendlies"

INTERIOR   OUTSIDE

OUTPOST NUMBER NINE
(DETAIL)

Outpost Number Nine is a typical High Plains military outpost of the days following the Battle of the Little Big Horn, and is the home of Easy Company. It is not a "fort"; an official fort is the headquarters of a regiment. However, it resembles a fort in its construction.

The birdseye view shows the general layout and orientation of Outpost Number Nine; features are explained in the Key.

The detail shows a cross-section through the outpost's double walls, which ingeniously combine the functions of fortification and shelter.

The walls are constructed of sod, dug from the prairie on which Outpost Number Nine stands, and are sturdy enough to withstand an assault by anything less than artillery. The roof is of log beams covered by planking, tarpaper, and a top layer of sod. It also provides a parapet from which the outpost's defenders can fire down on an attacking force.

EASY COMPANY
AND THE WHISKEY TRAIN

one ─────────────────────

This year, spring came slowly to the High Plains of Wyoming Territory. The deep snows remained late in the shaded draws. To the north and west, in the Bighorns and the Absarokas, the breakup was especially heavy when it finally came, with the Greybull and Snake Rivers chock full and spilling over their banks, the green-gray water rushing down to the south country, carrying branches and sometimes whole trees, their upended roots racing along with the great chunks of ice. All through the territory, the hard winter gave ground reluctantly as it met the young spring in the arrival of geese, in the newly dropped buffalo calves, in the shedding coats of the horses, and in the grass that was beginning to sweeten on the softening prairie.

South of the Bighorn Mountains and about a day's ride east of the Absarokas, a mounted infantry patrol stretched across the bare plain. First Lieutenant Matt Kincaid rode at the head of the column, his tall silhouette firm yet not rigid in his McClellan saddle, his sharp, careful eyes searching the land before him. He was in his thirties, overage in grade, serving his second tour of duty in the Army of the West; he was a man of good humor and no nonsense, as his fellow officers and the enlisted men under him could attest. Kincaid's blue eyes could laugh, but they could also cut a man to size without a word being spoken. The big bay gelding beneath him was frisky now as the sun moved down toward the edge of the sky, and the chill of late afternoon slipped across the big land.

It had been a fairly routine patrol. The telegraph wire to regimental headquarters had been down, and Captain Warner Conway, commanding Easy Company at Outpost Number Nine, had called for a squad to ride out and repair it. Routine. The Indians of the area cut the wire with tedious frequency; the line was down nearly as often as it was operative.

But as the men were mounting up, an excited young homesteader came pounding in from the north with news that the Sioux were sweeping down from Little Cat Creek like a scythe. They had set fire to Hanrahan's, at Packhorse Butte, and God knew where they were now.

Conway, a veteran of such grim alarms, bore in mind the possibility of exaggeration owing to the fear that an Indian attack invariably provoked. The rider was a young boy—green to the country, too—and this had to be taken into account. You could never really be sure how much was fact and how much was "extra," as Easy's civilian scout, Windy Mandalian, liked to put it. The Little Cat Creek Sioux had been at peace since the start of negotiations for the new treaty, and there had been no rumor or gossip of any trouble through Windy's grapevine; this suggested the possibility either of exaggeration or mistaken identity. In any event, action was called for, and Conway ordered out a bigger patrol, with Matt Kincaid and Mandalian.

By the time Kincaid, Windy, and the patrol reached Hanrahan's, the marauders were long gone. Conway's hunch had been right; the damage was small. The hostiles had burnt a haystack, and had ransacked the kitchen under the furious eyes of the homesteaders. But no one had been killed or molested, Hanrahan himself being the only casualty. The bony homesteader had suffered a split cheek from an arrow, having reached for his Henry rifle at the wrong moment. When the patrol rode up he was cursing the loss of his haystack, which the hostiles had obviously fired in order to distract the homesteaders while they entered the house.

"Cut Hand," Windy said.

"Himself, or his warriors?" Matt asked.

"I'd say his people, but he could've been with them. The question is why. The Sioux have been at peace this good while. Why such a sudden breakout?"

"Hanrahan said he thought there was whiskey," Matt said.

3

"That could explain it. Except usually when they can't handle the stuff they go berserk, really raise hell, not just like this here."

After leaving Hanrahan's, they checked two other homesteaders and one rancher with a few dozen head of cattle in the area, but the Sioux had not visited them; they had vanished. Evidently the attack on Hanrahan's had been their only strike. About two miles farther to the west, they found the pole where the telegraph wire had been cut. Stretch Dobbs, six feet seven inches tall, climbed up to splice the wire.

"Now we can go back home and pick up all the bad news they been trying to tell us," Windy said.

The patrol had stopped now to let the horses blow and drink at a little creek at the edge of the meadow, a few hundred yards from the newly spliced telegraph line.

Kincaid watched Windy Mandalian cutting a generous chew of tobacco with his big skinning knife. "See anything out on the flanks, old-timer?"

"I seen it is Cut Hand for sure."

"How so?" Matt looked carefully at the long, lean scout slouching in his comfortable stock saddle on the chunky blue roan.

Windy leaned forward and spat just as the roan stuck out his right foreleg and bent to rub his long nose against it. Matt Kincaid grinned at the horse's apparent knowledge of its rider's movements. Indeed, the man and the horse, as Warner Conway had more than once pointed out, appeared to be a single entity, so attuned were they to each other.

"On account of some tracks I seen yonder, leading toward Little Cat Creek. And also on account of this here." Windy held out his hand, in which lay a small round silver medallion with the head of George Washington stamped on it. It was attached to a leather string.

Kincaid examined it carefully. "How do you figure this means Cut Hand?"

"Cut Hand visited Washington about five years ago with some other Sioux and Cheyenne chiefs. Somebody there—maybe the President, for all I know—gave him a big medal, along with a mess of small ones like this here for his headmen. I have seen the big one. He wears it under his shirt, right next to his skin."

"Where did you find this?"

"Yonder." Windy nodded his head in the general direction from which they had come. "Same horses as was at Hanrahan's."

Kincaid turned around in his saddle. "Sergeant, tell the men they can dismount."

"Yes, sir." The stocky, weathered Gus Olsen, First Platoon's regular sergeant, lifted himself in his saddle and barked the order.

With great relief, the men swung to the ground.

"Christ, my balls are in little pieces from that fucking McClellan," Private Malone announced. The big Irishman stepped gingerly away from his horse as he unbuttoned his fly to relieve himself.

"I took mine off and kept 'em in my pocket," Stretch Dobbs said. His remark brought a ripple of laughter from the dismounting men. Pop Fegan, the senior soldier of Easy Company, belched loudly. "Cold coffee," he said, "on empty stomach make sick man."

Only a chuckle rose in answer to this observation. Pop, prematurely gray, held seniority in years and the company's top score in marksmanship—he was a sharpshooter—but not in soldiering. He was the eternal private, grumblingly agreeable. He liked cigars, whiskey, and sleep. He could shoot the eyelash off a diving hawk, or so Windy Mandalian put it, allowing that the only marksman who could beat Pop was himself. Other than his marksmanship, Pop had never revealed any other singular characteristics. In physical appearance he was utterly plain. Mostly, Pop was durable.

Pop Fegan, like everybody else, had chosen the moment to relieve himself. Unfortunately he had not realized how close he was standing to Malone until, laughing at his own observation about coffee on a cold stomach, he swung his body a little and the big Irishman yelled and jumped at the same time.

"Goddammit, Pop, you fire your Springfield like you fire that goddamn hose of yours, the Sioux'll cut you off at the pockets."

This little byplay elicited a sharp reprimand from Olsen.

"Cut the shit, you assholes! We're still in hostile country!"

Kincaid had been examining the little silver medallion that Windy had handed him.

"Pretty, ain't it?" the scout said, and he pursed his lips up tight beneath his nose, wrinkling his forehead at the same time.

Matt was looking at him. "You've got something on your mind, you old buzzard."

"I don't hear you saying, 'Let's pay a visit to Cut Hand,'" Windy replied, and he shoved his chew into the side of his mouth, where it bulged his cheek out like a ball.

"As I said," Matt repeated, "you've got to have something on your mind besides hair."

"That medal was hanging from a bullberry bush."

"You mean you couldn't have missed it if it had stood up and hit you."

"That's just what it did do."

"Funny how it got off somebody's neck and onto that bush."

"That is exactly what this old scout is saying." Windy lowered one eyelid in a slow wink.

"You're suggesting that there's more here than just a simple raid to let off some of the usual spring pressure."

"Matt, old boy, that Cut Hand is one of the smartest—if not *the* smartest—of them 'simple, primitive natives' I have ever smoked a peace pipe with."

In the next moment, at a signal from Kincaid, Gus Olsen's hard voice cracked across the meadow. "Mount up!"

"Christ," muttered Malone, settling into his saddle. "I'm even looking forward to Rothausen's grub. I can feel snow coming."

He looked over at Pop Fegan, and then his eyes slid past the older man to another grayheaded soldier—Easy Company's newest recruit, who might easily have

7

been older than Pop, though it didn't say so on his records.

"Hanging in there, Pony boy?" Malone asked when he saw the older man wince as his crotch settled into the McClellan yet again.

"Doing fine, Malone." The voice of the thin, wiry man with the long face was unexpectedly deep.

"That ain't no pony express horse," Corporal Wojensky observed as he kneed his bay gelding into line.

Pony Tom Tooth, former express rider for Russell, Majors, and Waddell smiled. "It ain't the horse," he said. "It's the saddle—if it can be called a saddle." He winced again, and hoped he wasn't getting piles.

Pony Tom felt a sense of relief at the mild funning. He had taken a lot of pains with the men and first sergeant of Easy Company to establish a past history as a Pony Express rider out of St. Joe, which he had indeed been, though that was more than sixteen years ago, and he'd been a boy. Later, as he told it, he'd been a bank clerk in California. The first story, which was true, supported the second, which was not.

Suddenly, Dobbs' alarmed voice called out, "Where the hell are we heading, boys? This ain't the way back to Number Nine."

At this point, Kincaid rode back down the line. "We are heading for Cut Hand's camp on Little Cat Creek," he said. "I expect every man to be on full alert. We can encounter hostiles at any moment. I want no talking, no smoking. Check your weapons, your spare ammunition." He turned to Olsen, who was riding

8

beside him. "Sergeant, put an extra man on point and on either flank. We're getting some snow."

When he rode back to the head of the column, he found that Windy Mandalian had ridden out to join one of his Delaware scouts.

Pony Tom felt the first wet snowflake on his forehead. The sky had darkened swiftly, and now, as the patrol rode through a draw thick with crackwillow, all felt the frigid blast of the night rolling across the plain, and the stinging needles of snow.

Pony Tom Tooth huddled into his uniform. Yes, he was thinking, maybe for a change his decision had been the correct one. Maybe the Army of the West was indeed the best place to hide.

two ─────────────────────────

The area between the Bighorn Mountains and the South Pass, which it was Easy Company's duty to patrol, was as big, as difficult, as boring, and as dangerous and exciting as anything Captain Warner Conway ever wanted to encounter.

This was his sector, the territory the army wanted policed. In it were Arapaho, Cheyenne, and Sioux, along with some Shoshone, Crow, and a few others. But the native population was not all. There were settlers, homesteaders, sodbusters, farmers, and ranchers, not to mention a motley riffraff of gamblers, whores, and gunmen.

There were also some small towns. But mainly there

were always people, with their problems, complaints, hatreds, fears, violence, and, not infrequently, kindness.

There were always people at Outpost Number Nine. Besides the soldiers, there were civilians such as the hostlers and the sutler. And there were the transient Indians, usually at Tipi Town, just outside the post, to the northeast. There were also those who were passing through, notably freighters and drummers, or an occasional emigrant train that had strayed off the trail west.

Outpost Number Nine was situated on a large, rolling table of land about five to six thousand feet above sea level. These were the High Plains, whose brown grass stretched as far as a man could see. Only in the spring was it green for a short while, but this particular spring there was still snow covering most of the ground.

On that rolling prairie, Outpost Number Nine sat on one of the higher knolls that afforded an unobstructed view for about a quarter-mile in all directions. It was advantageous for the defenders, but tough on anyone trying to mount an attack.

Although constructed as a fortification, Outpost Number Nine was not a fort. Army records listed Easy Company's home as an outpost. Yet it served the same functions as the regimental fort, some distance to the east as the telegraph poles traveled: it defended its occupants against attack by hostile forces, and served as a standing symbol of the notion of Manifest Destiny.

Constructed of timber, tarpaper, and prairie sod, not to mention spit, urine, and profanity, this remarkably functional edifice on a rammed-earth foundation, sitting right out there in the middle of no place at all, was home to the men—and the very few women—of Easy Company.

Now, in the hour before dawn, the snow that had been slicing down in long needles turned into a penetrating drizzle. It got colder; but then, as the eastern sky began to lighten a little, the rain stopped, and suddenly the new day broke over the wide prairie, the first rays of the sun piercing the leaden sky, washing along the eastern wall of Number Nine, reaching shortly the roof of the enlisted men's barracks, the officers' quarters, the messhall and stables, until at last it found the window of Easy Company's orderly room.

The orderly room was deserted at that moment, until the door leading from the CO's office opened and Captain Warner Conway walked in.

For a moment the commanding officer just stood there, wondering when Kincaid and the patrol would get back. The telegraph was obviously working, for a soldier had appeared a few moments before to report that a message was coming through at the telegraph shack next to the main gate in the east wall of the outpost. First Sergeant Ben Cohen, next to whose desk Conway now stood, had sent the company clerk, Corporal Bradshaw, known as Four Eyes, to wait for the completed message and bring it back, along with a pot of fresh coffee from the mess.

The orderly room door opened now, and Four Eyes entered with a steaming granitewear coffeepot in one hand and a small sheet of foolscap in the other. He

13

handed the paper to Conway and placed the coffeepot on Cohen's desk. Cohen poured two cups of coffee and handed one to Conway, who took it absently, his eyes fixed on the piece of flimsy paper in his other hand. His forehead creased in a frown as he read. Cohen and the bespectacled Bradshaw exchanged a worried glance. The thoughts of both men were the same: *Damn the telegraph anyway. When it breaks down or the wire gets cut, somebody has to risk his neck to fix it, and when it's working, it only brings bad news...*

It was the Moon of the Red Grass Appearing—April— and the camp on Little Cat Creek was astir with activity. The crier had gone through the camp, calling the people to the brilliant new day. It had suddenly become spring, and while the blue asters and yellow goldenrod and some other bright flowers were not yet in evidence, the buds on the cottonwoods and box elders lining the creek showed clean and soft against the light blue sky of the beginning day. Smoke rose slowly from the smoke holes of the tipis, and there was a smell of cooking meat, the barking of dogs. A girl child stood outside her father's tipi and watched a jay balancing on a bullberry bush. A young man who had just washed in the creek stood in the light of the rising sun, letting its warmth dry him, droplets of water glistening on his bronzed body. A jay called raucously, and another answered. From the pony herd came the sound of a grazing bell, as the animals cropped at the sweet new bunch grass.

14

Cut Hand was still seated outside his lodge, on the blanket that Whispering Deer, his youngest wife, had placed there for him. From here he had watched the night leaving the sky, the morning star rising, while the dawn came once again to the earth. He sat without moving, listening with his whole being. He was listening to the air, to the beings of the earth, and to the life inside himself.

"Be attentive!" the Grandfathers and the Thunder Beings had told him. "Hear the spirit of life. Listen only to the Great Spirit who is in everything." This they had told him long ago, when he was still a boy and had had his vision on Blue Mountain. Now a man of sixty-five winters, he remembered. Always it was necessary to remember.

He remembered as he sat smoking, waiting for the light to inhabit the whole sky, his eyes on the morning star.

Yesterday the bluecoats had come—as he had expected, for he had planned it. His scouts had told him of the one named Windy finding the little round silver picture where he had told Young Bear to leave it. Young Bear and Cricket had also told him of the visit the bluecoats had made to the man whose grass had been fired.

It had pained him to hear of the burning of the grass stack, and of the arrow sent into the man's face. Yes, the man had reached for his rifle, but Young Bear and Cricket and the others had been filled with whiskey. Then, when the madness had worn off, they had come to Cut Hand and told him of it, though not with strong voices, but reluctantly, their defiance still stronger than their honesty.

Yes, he thought, the words were often true, but the tone of voice, the face, the movement of the body told the lie. In this, he reflected, the Real People were little different than the *Wasichus*, the whites. Both revealed their true natures. Only the *Wasichus* seemed always to lie. The white men he knew were mostly soldiers, yet the soldiers said that it was the other whites, the ones in Washington, who gave orders and wrote things on paper, the treaties they never kept. The soldiers were not so bad. They were at least men who could fight. Of course, their way was different, for they fought far away from their families, their wives and children, and their old people, while the Sioux always had their people with them. And, too, the whites fought only to kill. They killed the Real People as they killed the buffalo.

Now he quieted his thoughts, deciding not to let them take him, bringing his mind back to the meeting with the lieutenant soldier and Windy, the scout for the bluecoats. He had told the lieutenant, Kincaid, and Windy that Young Bear and Cricket and their little band would pay the man for his stacked grass. They would hunt for him so that he would have meat. It was surely better than going to the Iron House at the big fort. Young Bear and the others had not liked it, but the elders had agreed that it was needed to keep the peace with the *Wasichus*, for they, the whites, were far too many.

He had gambled with the silver picture, knowing

that the bluecoats would come to Little Cat Creek anyway, for they knew it was the Sioux at the haystack man's place. So he, Cut Hand, had the medal put on the bush for the whites to find it, in this way telling them that he was turning to them, trusting them. For he needed them to stop the whiskey wagons. It was this that held his attention now. If the brown fire came to the People, it would truly bring bad times.

He could tell that Kincaid had been pleased. He had listened carefully, asking good questions about the whiskey and the men who sold it to the Sioux, saying that it was wrong, but that it was to be expected. The whiskey wagons came into the country because there was no other way the stinging water could be brought to the whites out here in the open land—but that it must not come on the reservation. That was against the Washington lawmaking, and so it was bad. Cut Hand could not understand why something was considered bad because it was against what the *Wasichus* called the law, rather than because it made everyone sick and crazy.

Yes, it was difficult to know how the white man thought, how he saw things. Even so, he tried. With difficulty he read their newspapers, the stories of happenings in the white man's world. He had even read about the fight with Yellow Hair Custer at the Greasy Grass. Not one of the whites had lived to tell the story, yet they had told of it in their newspaper. He could not understand that.

Still, he wished to learn their ways. It was necessary, for he had to help the People. They were in the white man's world now; they were prisoners of war. But they must never forget the other world. And that other world must be kept alive, so that one day it could flower again. It was why he had told Young Bear to hang the silver picture on the bullberry bush.

"That's how I figure Cut Hand had that medal hung on that bush," Windy Mandalian was saying as he leaned against the wall in Captain Conway's office.

Conway, seated at his desk, looked across at Matt Kincaid. "I certainly can't blame him for being fearful of the whiskey," he said. "It's just a plain fact that the Indians can't handle the stuff."

"Some whites ain't too good at it neither," Windy observed.

"Not counting anyone present," Kincaid added with a laugh.

Windy sniffed. "It's a cinch that if the white man's bullets don't get 'em, the white man's booze will." The scout detached himself from the wall he was leaning against, and stepping briskly over to Conway's desk, he spat vigorously into the spittoon on the floor next to it.

"Windy, you ought to watch it when you move that fast. You don't want to let that wall fall down," Matt said as he leaned forward, coming up off the seat of his chair to accept the cigar offered by his commanding officer. "Thank you, sir."

Now there was a short silence while the two soldiers each bit the ends off their cigars and lighted them.

18

Conway had taken three luxurious draws on his cigar, his eyes following the plume of smoke rising to the ceiling as he leaned back in his swivel chair.

"Well, that's settled. They'll bring Hanrahan some elk, buffalo, whatever, and the hay situation will become history." Conway laid his cigar down in the fancy ashtray that someone had brought him from the Stockgrower's Club in Kansas City. His eyes were directly on his adjutant.

Matt suddenly had that uneasy feeling in the pit of his stomach that he always got when he knew bad news was coming.

"Captain, I can tell you've got something for me."

Conway chuckled. "Guess you know me pretty well, Matt."

"Regiment?"

"Who else?"

Conway studied the back of his hand, then lifted his eyes to his adjutant. Warner Conway considered Matt Kincaid the model of what a top soldier should be. He fully deserved the captaincy that Washington owed him, and more. Yet Conway knew what a rough time he'd have running Easy Company without his first lieutenant.

"Trouble, trouble," muttered Windy Mandalian, and he lifted his battered hat and resettled it on his head, squatting now with his elbows on his knees, his long, bony hands hanging down from his bent wrists.

"Trouble," Conway mused. "The point is, Regiment has got a ticklish job they want done, and as usual, they've kicked it down to us. They say they want my best man for the job, and Matt, you're it."

Matt Kincaid felt the weakness of the grin on his face as he said wryly, "I will try to take that as a compliment, sir."

"Matt, I'll lay it right out. It's one of Regiment's shit details. What the army brass refers to in their droll way as 'housekeeping.'"

"I'm ready for the worst, Captain," Matt said, his good humor returning.

Conway sighed. "This one came over the wire yesterday." His lips tightened. "Just after you repaired the break." His eyes moved to the wall map behind Kincaid. "I did try to get Regiment to understand that the problem was theirs, not ours—but you know how far I got."

"Rank has its privileges."

"It does. I even suggested they send a ranker from one of the forts north or west of here."

"How did that go down, sir?"

A tight grin appeared on Conway's face. "They simply told me that Easy Company was being given the assignment because there would be less chance of any repercussions if the job was handled by an isolated outfit." He paused, then continued, "If there's one thing the Custer affair taught them, Matt, it's the power of civilians when they get stirred up."

"Sir, I must say that by now I am dying with curiosity, if not with a certain dread..."

Windy shifted his right leg forward while remaining in his hunkered position, Matt looked down at the backs of his hands, resting on his knees, and Warner Conway reached for his cigar.

At a knock on the door, Conway said, "Come."

It was Sergeant Cohen who appeared in the doorway. "Message from Regiment, sir. They're requesting an immediate reply to yesterday's dispatch."

"Thank you, sergeant."

Cohen shifted his thick shoulders as he turned and left the office.

Conway picked up a paper that was lying on his desk, though his eyes were on Kincaid.

"The story is, a civilian has reported to regimental headquarters that Colonel Jonathan Blue, commanding Fort Stambaugh, rode out with a detachment of men and attacked and destroyed a wagon train hauling whiskey into the territory. This action took place at Whistle Creek, southwest of Muddy Gap. Since Colonel Blue was acting without orders, Regiment has requested that Easy Company rein him down. I don't have to tell you how unpopular Colonel Blue is in the army. He smashed a couple of saloons back in Kansas; that's why they shipped him out here."

"Jesus!" Windy muttered.

"Blue won't allow any drinking on any post he commands."

"Not even beer?" Matt asked.

"Not even beer."

"How does he get away with that shit?" Windy wanted to know.

"He invokes the 1853 prohibition law. It's still on the books, though no one even remembers it."

"Jesus!" Windy said again.

"But the colonel was acting on his own initiative, wasn't he, sir?"

Conway nodded. "He was—but the colonel has friends in high places. At the same time, headquarters has had enough of his nonsense." Conway's face was hard as he said, "Matt, your assignment is Fort Stambaugh."

"And the orders, sir?"

"You are to stop Colonel Blue. Regiment wants him stopped. But Regiment also wants it done without anyone—that means army or civilian—knowing about it. And I, of course, want Easy Company to come out with very clean hands."

A strange silence fell over the office then.

It was Windy Mandalian who broke it. "Well, Matt, old son, all I can say is, you never should of spliced that goddamn telegraph wire in the first place."

three _____

It had all happened so simply and with such suddenness that nobody could possibly have imagined such an eventuality in advance.

It had been a very warm day. Slowly the mule-drawn wagon moved across the floor of the wide valley. It was a big wagon, heavily loaded with barrels and crates filled with bottles—the barrels for the various sutlers' stores ahead, the bottles for army officers in residence at the forts and outposts. The wheels of the heavy wagon cut deep into the softening spring earth.

Two aged men sat on the wagon box directly behind the mules, while a third man, equally historic, rode a short distance ahead on an ancient horse with a body that sagged like a hammock. Overhead, the white sun beat down evenly on men and animals alike.

"Gettin' to be a short spring," said the man holding the leather lines of the mule team. His tobacco-stained beard quivered as he spat lazily onto the rump of the nearest mule. "Shit take it, I could use me a drink."

The mules bobbed their heads with each step; the man seated beside the driver nodded as he dozed. Herkimer Bill Fall, on the horse about a hundred yards ahead, now turned back to the wagon.

"Creek up ahead," he said as he approached. "Good place to let 'em blow. Give us a rest."

"Good enough." Barney Smith, the driver, nodded in agreement, then turned his head toward his companion on the wagon box. "Wake up, Clarence. We're comin' into San Francisco!"

The dozing man stirred, and his lips began to move, his tongue licking out along the edge of his beard. His eyes were still closed as he spoke:

"Not much you can do about the weather, Barney," he said, answering his companion's observation of several moments ago. "Shit, that's all there is out here anyways." And opening his eyes slowly, he spat, also at the rump of the nearest mule, but his aim was less true than Barney Smith's had been, the spittle falling onto the singletree instead of on its intended target.

In a new silence now, the three men approached the creek, which was lined with willows and cottonwoods. They all carried weapons—sidearms and Winchesters—and were old hands by now at hauling whiskey from the Union Pacific tracks, south of Buffalo Crossing, up to the pass in the Medicine Bow Range at Muddy Gap. There had been brief skirmishes with the Indians, but nothing serious, the hostiles showing more caution than resolve as a result of the army's presence at nearby Fort Stambaugh. More than once, the whiskey men had paid off the attackers with a bottle or two of the brown fire. Thus a working relationship with the Arapahoes, the Shoshones, and some stray Sioux now and again, had been established in the area.

"We'll make it to the Gap come nighfall," Herkimer Bill Fall predicted hoarsely. "We can take a short break." Years past, Herkimer had been shot in the throat making a break out of Folsom Prison, and had spoken with difficulty ever since.

Barney Smith's eyes opened wide. They were pale blue, their whites streaked with red lines. A hole appeared in his thick yellow-gray beard. Herkimer Bill realized the old geezer was laughing.

"If you reckon you can stay astride that there crowbait," he said, and winked hugely at Herkimer Bill.

Herkimer ignored the thrust. "Maybe if Doc there can stay awake, we might make it. Ain't it his turn to skin them mules?"

Barney Smith sawed on the lines, and when the team stopped, he wrapped the reins around the brake handle.

Presently, seated in the shade, the three oldsters addressed themselves to jerked beef, hardtack, canned peaches, and some of their own liquid merchandise.

Clarence Lightfoot, however, refused the whiskey. He claimed not to be a drinking man, favoring instead a libation of his own making known as Dr. Clarence Lightfoot's Sure-Shot Panacea, a patent medicine he had hawked just about all over the northern parts of the great American West—until enraged citizens in Cardew City had caught up with him and ridden him out of town on a rail. Yet such was Doc's faith in his Sure-Shot Panacea that he continued to make it from its secret formula, a large percentage of which was indeed pure alcohol; and in fact he seldom drank anything else. Doc did occasionally hawk his medicine, but without the devotion of former years. He hoped to return at some future date to full-time trumpeting of his fabled product: "The greatest family medicine of the age! Taken internally, it cures cholera, burns, swelled joints, boils, ringworm, indigestion. It will put an end to consumption, decline, asthma, bronchitis, wasting of the flesh, whooping cough, colds, and night sweats. Have you a sickly child? A lame horse? Dr. Clarence Lightfoot's miracle is made from pure vegetable compounds; it is the great American painkiller, the people's friend!" He intoned the fabulous litany to himself several times a day. Ah, such a comfort!

Doc greatly enjoyed the polished, ringing sentence. His two months as a student at Harvard University had stirred in him a love of language, learning—and alcohol. Somehow, in that short sojourn among the halls of ivy, he had acquired the final polish, the legitimate

26

touch of "education" that would determine his role in life. His career was inevitable.

Indeed, if it hadn't been for that jasper in Cardew City, with his trick donkey, he'd still be hawking Sure-Shot Panacea from his painted wagon; but that damned old trapper had right there given a shot of the elixir to his donkey, who had promptly let out a tremendous bray and keeled over with his legs and tail stretched out as stiff as ramrods. Doc had narrowly escaped a lynching by the irate mob. It was a long time later, and quite by chance, that he'd discovered how the old trapper had slickered him with his trained animal. But by then his tainted reputation had spread like a prairie fire, and he'd had to switch to another line of endeavor. Drawn to the cards, he discovered that he was not born to win. His losses were disastrous. Nor was love his province. A brief marriage to a lady gambler named One-Eye Annie had ended sourly. Now, at an advanced age, he'd been reduced to riding shotgun on a load of whiskey. A helluva note!

Barney Smith had brought out a deck of cards, and while they enjoyed their victuals and libation, they played a few hands of stud. The three were in good shape as they started up again.

"We'll make Muddy Gap pretty directly," Barney Smith said. He had been a former sutler at an army fort in Nebraska, and his experience was considered useful to the whiskey-train enterprise.

While Barney had been unsuccessful in his attempts to feather his own nest at army expense, his native enterprise had shown itself in his ability to extract himself from nasty situations as clean as the well-known whistle. In short, he was resourceful.

Scratching his beard, Barney looked back at Herkimer Bill Fall, who was just mounting his horse.

Herkimer was a stringy man with a long face that seemed to match his gravelly voice. He dreamed of making a big strike and retiring to ranch life. A former road agent, he had been a lifer in Folsom prison in California, having been captured by Wells, Fargo agents after holding up the Oroville stage. But he'd eventually become a model prisoner and had earned a governor's pardon.

They had just rounded a high cutbank. The two men were dozing on the wagon box, Herkimer Bill riding beside them on his aged horse, dreaming of a successful holdup of the Union Pacific, when, without the slightest warning, a detachment of soldiers rode out of a grove of box elders and straight at them, the officer in charge ordering the wagon to halt.

It didn't take more than a moment for the three whiskey-train men to discover that the colonel who now confronted them was a man with a mission.

"You men are under arrest!" he announced.

"Under arrest!" Barney Smith's jaw dropped to his chest as he stared in total disbelief at the little man on the big white horse.

"That is correct, mister! You are transporting whiskey across Indian territory in violation of the law."

"Law!" cried the three in unison. Herkimer Bill's

horse caught the agitation and began to spook.

"The law, I say! It is prohibited to bring whiskey onto Indian lands, sir. That law has been on the books since 1853!"

"But we never..."

The colonel's white stallion had started to prance, maybe catching the mood from Herkimer Bill's crow-bait, who clearly wanted to buck, but didn't have the strength.

"Stop that!" snapped the colonel, slapping his mount with his quirt. "Stop it, I say!"

The colonel was a very short man. This was obvious even in the saddle. Indeed, almost everyone was taller than he, but as everyone who had ever met him said, he more than made up for his lack of height. He was in his fifties, though in good condition. His black mustache was trim, his uniform crisp and gleaming. His face shone. Some people said he looked like a pigeon.

"You talking about that prohibition law, Colonel?" Doc asked, coming in easy now, one eye almost closed as he squinted curiously at the army officer.

"I am, sir. I am here to uphold and, yes, to enforce that law. For your information, I am Colonel Jonathan Blue, commanding at Fort Stambaugh. You men will be held under arrest until you are tried by court-martial."

"Colonel, how come you are so all-fired certain we have got whiskey aboard here?"

"My God, man, you're stinking up the whole territory!" Jonathan Blue's aquiline nose wrinkled in disgust as he turned suddenly in his saddle, looking like a small, brightly painted toy. But there was nothing toylike about his orders.

"Sergeant Fowler!"

"Sir!" A swarthy-looking man rode up.

"Do your duty, Sergeant!"

Sergeant Fowler's brown face paled as he saluted. "Yes, sir." Fowler turned in his saddle, his whole attitude rigid with reluctance.

"Sergeant, that is a direct order!"

"Williams! Gerhard! Stronski! Your service hatchets!"

Three men rode forward, untying their service hatchets from their saddles as they did so.

"Dismount!"

The men swung to the ground. In total horror, Doc, Barney, and Herkimer Bill watched as the three executioners stepped up to the wagon and began smashing their hatchets into the whiskey barrels. As the rich amber fluid began to flow, a gasp broke from the three whiskey-train men; but the soldiers who were still mounted suffered in funereal silence. The crates were broken into next, and the bottles smashed against the wagon wheels. Only the mules, standing humbly in their traces, appeared unmoved by the carnage. Strangely, a case of Doc's Sure-Shot Panacea was spared, Doc flinging himself on the case and screaming that it contained medicine.

"We'll see!" Colonel Blue promised, and he barked out an order for the men to be thorough.

"Every drop!" The colonel's words were as hard

and cold as the man delivering them. His small round face gleamed with satisfaction, as though those dark features were lacquered.

"Colonel, sir, you don't want to save *any?*" Sergeant Fowler sat his horse, his body limp, his eyes filled with pain at what was being wrought before their horrified gaze.

Even before he finished speaking, his query was lost in a hurricane of invective that all but swept him out of his saddle.

"You bloody fool! It is a hatchetation, Fowler! It is not for the weak and puling, my man! It is the will of the Lord! The demon rum is the tool of Lucifer! Be done with it, you fool!" The colonel paused, saliva flecking his lips, his little body vibrating as he almost bounced in his saddle under the force of his own words. "Drunkenness!" And he held up his forefinger. It was very short, Doc Lightfoot noticed. "Drunkenness, men, is the egg from which all vices are hatched!"

"Jesus God!" murmured Barney Smith, cringing at what his eyes beheld. It was enough, he told himself, to turn the blackest heart to prayer.

Colonel Blue was a man who had always been ruled by impatience. Suddenly he kicked his big white horse forward and, seizing a hatchet from the hand of a surprised soldier, began to lay about one of the remaining crates of whiskey, leaning far out of his saddle to do so.

"A bottle is a drunkard's purse!" he cried now, dropping the hatchet and grabbing a bottle of whiskey. Hurling it into the air, he swiftly drew his Schofield

31

Smith & Wesson and shot it before it hit the ground; whiskey and shards of glass showered down, bringing a groan from the three who huddled near their totally patient mules.

"That is sacrilege, pure and simple," intoned Barney Smith. "The Lord will not be pleased."

Blue, overhearing, swept his hard face toward the teamster. "You may use the Lord's name in vain, mister, but I shall quote from the immortal Shakespeare: 'Oh! that men should put an enemy in their mouths to steal away their brains.'"

He had no sooner spoken than Herkimer Bill's horse found energy in some miraculous way and started to spook even more. Backing up suddenly, it slipped and almost went down, but Bill kept his seat. The Colonel, however, was less fortunate. He had taken another hatchet from one of the soldiers, and at that moment was breaking into the last crate of whiskey. But the antics of Herkimer's horse frightened the big white stallion, who spun, his long teeth snapping at the old nag. The maneuver caught the colonel off guard. He had been leaning far out of his saddle, chopping at the crate, and all at once he fell right into the wagon.

Sergeant Fowler and a private dashed to his rescue, but the colonel rose unhurt, glaring at them, his crisp uniform dark with whiskey; yet not for one instant did he lose his incredible dignity. A massive silence fell as, refusing aid, he dismounted stiffly from the wagon and regained his McClellan saddle on the white stallion.

It was all over. Reeking of whiskey, Colonel Jonathan Blue rode at the head of the column of whey-faced soldiers and the three prisoners, the whiskey wagon bringing up the rear. No funeral had ever been more somber than the procession that finally reached Fort Stambaugh.

That evening, Colonel Blue took a very long bath. Sergeant Fowler and the men turned for solace to their companions-in-arms, relating the terrible tidings of that day.

There was a gleam of hope. Barney Smith discovered that the sutler at Fort Stambaugh was an old friend, and a message was immediately dispatched to those quarters where it would receive understanding.

In no time at all, Colonel Jonathan Blue's action near Muddy Gap had swept through the Army of the West like a prairie fire.

"More like the pox than fire," noted an old-timer. "Fire is clean. What he done ain't *human*."

"The man is crazy, and that's all there is to it," was the summation offered through the terse lips of Colonel Thomas J. Bolling, Regimental Commander. "I've placed the situation in Conway's hands." He was talking to his adjutant. "Obviously, headquarters sent him West to get rid of him. We must do the same."

Captain Franklin Weatherby nodded. "Exactly, Colonel. I hope Conway will, er, handle the situation with discretion."

'Of course...of course." Bolling's irritation showed in his increased pace as he moved back and forth in his office. "I've heard of the man, you know," he told

Weatherby for the second time that morning. "Blue-nose is the name they gave him back at Fort Belcher, you know. Colonel Bluenose. Damn fool went out with a detachment and broke up several saloons in the nearby towns. That tore it."

"I know Captain Conway will do his best, sir," Weatherby said encouragingly.

"I don't want his best, Captain Weatherby. I want him to get rid of Colonel Bluenose!"

While a shudder ran through the Army of the West, at Outpost Number Nine the news of Colonel Blue-nose's depredations was received with the rage and loathing usually lavished on tales of torture and dis-memberment.

"The man is crazy," Malone said. "And that's all there is to it."

No one in Easy Company, of course, knew that the regimental commander, Colonel Bolling, had used those very words to state the situation, thus revealing with crystal clarity—for those with ears to hear—the underlying solidarity of the United States Army of the West.

Captain Warner Conway's words had been more colorful, however. "He is an asshole, pure and sim-ple." The captain was talking to Windy Mandalian. "Matt's going to have his hands full dealing with Blue. The stupid son of a bitch is AWOL in the first place."

"How you mean that?" Windy asked.

"He was acting without orders! No one cut him orders to go and smash up a civilian wagon train. And he left his post to do it. Sure, I know a lot of COs take things into their own hands, and not too seldom either—myself included—but that's in an emergency, that's when there's some sense to it."

Windy often discovered himself in the role of sounding-board for Conway or Kincaid; he rather enjoyed it, for he found army organization both quaint and astonishing. "So why don't the high mucky-mucks arrest him or somethin'?" Windy shifted his weight as he leaned against the wall next to the office window. "I mean, he's disobeying orders, right? So why don't they discipline him? Why does Easy Company have to get its ass wet?"

Warner Conway was asking himself the same questions, but he knew the answers. He knew that Windy knew the answers too, but it was necessary to say it.

"Because, first of all, there's that damned 1853 prohibition law." He held up his hand to restrain the reaction he saw in the scout. "Which nobody even remembers. Still, it's on the books. For Christ's sake, Windy, you know the army as well as I do. They pass the buck, and the buck has hit us. We're isolated. Nobody's going to notice us way out here. The main thing is not to make any problems for anyone higher up. I told this to Matt. Keep your nose clean and get rid of Blue, is what I told him."

"Jesus!" Windy snorted, jamming his hands deep into his trouser pockets. "That is a helluva note!"

"It is a hell of a note," Captain Warner Conway agreed, and he picked up his cigar, which had been resting in the ashtray on his desk. It was still alight.

Rising suddenly to his feet, he strode to the big wall map. "Stambaugh is in Smith's Gulch." He tapped at a spot on the map with his middle finger. "They call it a fort, but it's not an official designation; officially it's a camp, and it's not on the telegraph circuit." He turned back to Windy, who was still leaning against the wall next to the window.

"Interesting," the scout said.

Conway grinned. "I'm just telling you some background, you old reprobate. The army makes devious maneuvers, its wonders to perform. It's interesting that Blue was sent to Stambaugh—no telegraph, you see, and therefore very little communication with the outside world."

"I gotcha," Windy replied.

Conway walked back to his desk, but didn't sit down. "My God, can you imagine what it would be like out here if we couldn't get a drink!" He shook his head. "Of course, let's hand something to Blue. He doubtless figures he's doing his duty."

"Captain, there's a big difference between duty and suicide." And Windy lowered one eyelid in a slow wink.

"*Wasichus* are crazy," Cricket was saying as he and Young Bear regarded the carnage at Whistle Creek.

A half-dozen braves stood looking at the broken barrels, the smashed cases and bottles.

Young Bear looked west. "They have gone to the soldier fort."

"Truly," said Cricket, "it is hard to understand the *Wasichus*.

"And now Cut Hand says we must hunt meat for the ones with the hay mound. I do not understand it," Cricket said, running his fingers along one of the smashed barrels and then licking them.

"It is right," Young Bear said. "I do not like it, but it is right."

"Why is it right?"

"Because Cut Hand said it."

They stood looking at the wreckage for another long moment, then Young Bear turned and walked toward his pony, which had been chewing at the bark on a cottonwood tree.

In another moment the little band had mounted their ponies and ridden away, leaving the broken bottles, smashed cases and barrels, and spilled whiskey in the little clearing, with not even a buzzard circling overhead.

four ———————————

"Interesting, Lieutenant Kincaid. Most interesting that you pulled a tour of duty down in the Staked Plains." Colonel Jonathan Blue leaned back in his chair, his hand at the same time lifting his glass of water. "Was that under Colonel Gerritsen? I believe he's served a lot of his career in Texas."

"It was, sir. My immediate superior was Captain McNabb, however." Matt eyed the glass of water, glad that he had remembered to put a bottle of whiskey into his saddlebags before leaving Number Nine.

"Don't know him." Colonel Blue put down his empty glass, his eyes narrowing as he chose his words. "I knew Gerritsen slightly, back in Ohio. Good man.

Good officer." His stubby fingers drummed on the tabletop while the striker began removing the dishes. Matt noticed how hairy the backs of the colonel's fingers were.

They were in the commanding officer's quarters. Matt had arrived at Fort Stambaugh just that afternoon, accompanied by Corporal Wojensky and a private named Nolan. He had been greeted, not too warmly, by the colonel's adjutant, Captain Ned Forsyth, and an invitation to supper with the colonel and his wife came to him following his initial meeting with Blue. It had all been very correct.

He had told Blue and his adjutant that he was tracking a renegade Sioux named Young Bear, who had broken from his band on the reservation at Little Cat Creek and was thought to have headed in the direction of Smith's Gulch. It was a partial truth, since it was Young Bear who, with Cricket and the others, had set fire to Hanrahan's haystack.

"Lieutenant, I am at your disposal," the colonel had said cordially. "I think I should put it that my adjutant, Captain Forsyth, is at your disposal," he amended.

Matt watched Forsyth hide a wince by biting his lip. The gesture told him much of the situation at Stambaugh, and a good bit about Forsyth's character. There was something about the captain that Matt didn't trust. He was clearly arrogant, and his attitude even bordered on the patronizing toward his commanding officer. Blue, on the other hand, while clearly pompous and rigid, seemed to Matt to be living in his own private world, concerned only with impressing himself. Matt suspected that deep inside, the colonel might actually harbor a streak of decency. He wasn't so sure about Forsyth. He would have wagered that there'd be a number of bottles in the adjutant's room.

Kincaid was glad for the dinner invitation, for it offered an opportunity to study Blue. The closer he got to his actual assignment, the more he felt the impossibility of it. Regiment had no idea what they were asking. To rein down a full colonel commanding a fort—a firebrand to boot—without allowing a ripple in the always resonating gossip channels of the army, was to ask for a miracle. Blue unquestionably had friends, powerful allies in Washington. Politics, Conway had told Matt, had gotten Blue his place in the army, and politics would have to see to it that he remained. Sure, he'd been shipped out to Wyoming to get buried with his idiotic whiskey crusade, but the way it had been done only proved the existence of powerful connections in powerful places. Now the old boy might be having his last stand, though he was no Custer. Or was he?

But Matt had no opportunity to follow the thought through that evening as they supped in the colonel's quarters, for his attention was almost wholly captured by the presence of Miss Cynthia Blue. Both parents looked quite faded in comparison to the rose that had risen from their loins. The colonel and his lady could only be charitably described as plain. But beauty had lavished itself on the young girl. Matt judged her to be in her early twenties. Her cornsilk hair, combed down along the sides of her dewy face, was the perfect

41

setting for the large, deep brown eyes that gazed out on the world with exquisitely expressive innocence. Such innocence, Matt Kincaid realized, drove men to the basest thoughts, as well as to the highest dreams. Neither was it the perfection of her figure that was so enticing. It was her movement, her glance, her tinkling laughter and teasing lips. It was not in what she looked like, but in what she undoubtedly was that Kincaid realized that somebody, somewhere had blessed him with this impossible assignment.

"I'm so happy to hear about some of the rest of Wyoming, Lieutenant Kincaid," the delightful creature was saying, after Matt had described some of the country and towns to the north and east. "So far, all Mother and I have seen is the inside of this fort."

"Now Cynthia, that's not wholly true," her father chided. And for a moment, Matt saw a different Jonathan Blue under the shiny exterior of the officer.

"Daddy, we've been riding, Mother and I," she said, nodding her head at him as though he was a small child. "Yes? And riding. And riding. And riding..." And as she said the words quicker and quicker, she began to bounce a little in her chair, as though she were on a horse. The company all burst into a delighted laugh.

Even her mother smiled. Unfortunately her smile didn't become her, for Mrs. Blue had a long discolored patch—a birthmark—running down the side of her face and disappearing into the collar of her dress. She was overloaded with clothing, which made her look stocky, but it was difficult to tell. Her entire attitude was self-effacing, as though she were deliberately trying to make herself not only inconspicuous, but actually invisible. Probably, Matt thought, this was the result of the disfiguring birthmark. She was a careful, even a scrupulous hostess, who saw that her guests were provided with everything they desired, yet she hardly spoke or even seemed to exhibit much interest in her surroundings. As a result, everyone tended to ignore her, and she didn't seem to mind.

Matt was aware, though, that such people often actually controlled those around them more effectively than they could do through the direct exercise of power. He wondered if being married to a woman like Hester might have had a reverse effect on Blue from the usual, driving him not to drink, but to its opposite.

But the colonel was speaking again. Indeed, he had done little else for most of the evening. His voice was often harsh, revealing little sympathy for the subjects he was discussing, especially people.

"Your tour of duty down in Texas reminds me of something," he was saying. "Something that happened on the frontier, east of the Pecos. Funny story. I was at Fort Clinghorn at the time. Cattlemen were coming in pretty fast then. The stockmen, of course, eyed the lush greenland on the Indian reservations. Comanches. You'll recollect the Comanche chief, Yellow Bear," the colonel said. "What I'm telling you is a true story, fantastic as it might seem."

Kincaid heard the almost inaudible sigh that Forsyth emitted.

"I'd heard of him, sir. Yellow Bear was dead by

the time I got to the Staked Plains."

"Yes, he was. Anyhow, the Bear, as we called him, and another Indian named Horse-Runs-Swiftly were invited to Fort Worth by the cattlemen when they refused to sign a paper negotiating the grass. Yellow Bear roundly hated the whites, but Horse-Runs-Swiftly wasn't all that much against them. He was ready to make a deal. But both chiefs had to sign the paper. The cattlemen didn't press the issue, but instead put on a round of parties and banquets for the two chiefs.

"After the first day of this spirited social life, the Bear was pretty tired. So the old boy and Horse-Runs-Swiftly were taken to the town's best hotel and installed in the best suite. Everything went fine for the Bear, except he couldn't sleep. The flickering flame of the gaslight apparently bothered him. So he got up and blew it out. And then he had no trouble falling asleep."

The colonel paused to take another long drink of water, while Matt watched the changing expressions on his daughter's face. Obviously she had not heard the story before, for her surprise at the gaslight episode was clear, and her excited delight at the building drama. But equally obvious was the fact that Forsyth had heard the story, perhaps more than once. He could barely conceal his boredom and irritation.

"The next morning," continued Blue, "Yellow Bear's room was filled with gas. The old man was dead."

Kincaid glanced again at Hester Blue, who had remained expressionless throughout the narrative.

"The cattlemen staged a big funeral for the chief,

for they wanted to show the Comanches their good intentions. However, their efforts were received with less than warmth by the Indians. Yellow Bear, as they saw it, hadn't died from a bullet, or nobly in battle; he'd died from a mysterious 'bad air.' Because the other chief, Horse-Runs-Swiftly, had not also died, the Indians accepted the cattlemen's gifts and explanation about Yellow Bear's death with a good deal of suspicion. The point was, any hopes for their getting the grazing rights were just about doomed."

The colonel stopped again, gazing at Matt, at Forsyth, and at his daughter in turn. He did not look at his wife, who remained impassive, her eyes cast down.

"That certainly is the strangest story," Cynthia said. "But—is that all, Daddy?"

"No, it is not." Blue was looking down at the back of his hand, which was lying on the table before him. "It is not. They didn't know what to do. And what do people out here do when they don't know what to do? Eh?" A smile appeared on his shiny face. "They come to the army, that's what they do."

Kincaid grinned. Forsyth sighed a little less inaudibly, and Cynthia giggled.

"Enter the heroes!" the girl said, and burst into a teasing laugh.

"My dear, it was a ticklish situation," Blue remonstrated. "The Comanches, as Lieutenant Kincaid can tell you, are not the sort to be dallied with."

"Quite right, Colonel," Matt agreed.

"The Comanches were even in the mood—some of them—to avenge their chief's death."

"And so what did the army decide?" Cynthia asked. "I mean, the army saved the day, right? Hurrah!"

In spite of himself, her father had to smile. Even Forsyth grinned. Matt Kincaid thought he would explode with desire as the girl's eyes danced across his face.

"You see," the colonel resumed, "the Indians simply couldn't understand how 'bad air' could kill a man. We were desperate, let me tell you. But fortunately I remembered a jug of ammonia that we had in the officers' dayroom. I called in the head of the cattlemen and explained my idea, and he accepted the jug and went off with it to the Comanche camp. He took a couple of his men with him and asked the Indians to line up single file. Then, one by one, the Indians stepped up to the jug—as the cattleman suggested— and inhaled deeply. Of course, each Indian reeled back, coughing and gasping, wiping his eyes. But they were finally satisfied. If Yellow Bear had been a victim of this 'bad air,' he had died an honorable death."

"Bravo!" Cynthia cried with a big grin. "Daddy, you were a genius even back in Texas!"

At this, the entire company, with the exception of Hester Blue, burst into laughter.

Hester had risen to her feet and was now directing the striker in the clearing of the remainder of the dinner dishes from the table. The conversation continued for a few more moments, and Matt felt it was about time to take his departure.

"Colonel Blue, that's a nice story."

"It shows clearly, I do believe, the folly of imbibing

strong spirits," the colonel said. "If Yellow Bear had been sober, he would surely have smelled the gas in his room."

"Now then," Cynthia suddenly burst out, "I think I shall tell you a story about my first year in school, when I cured twelve of my schoolmates of leprosy."

"Cynthia!" Her mother's voice cut softly into the room. The word fell like velvet, yet nonetheless with a strength that a stronger tone could not have achieved.

"I'm sorry, Mother. I just got carried away."

"You mustn't tease your father."

"But it has been delightful, Mrs. Blue," Kincaid said, swiftly covering the moment. "I have had a wonderful evening."

In a few moments he had said goodbye to his host and two hostesses, and walked out to the parade. Hearing a step behind him, he turned. It was, of course, Ned Forsyth.

"How about a nightcap, Kincaid?"

"An excellent idea, Captain."

"The name is Ned when we're off duty."

"Another excellent idea—Ned."

The moon was full in an absolutely clear sky as they crossed to Forsyth's quarters. And as Matt had anticipated, Forsyth had seen to it that he had on hand an ample supply of liquor.

"I'm so glad you don't see eye to eye with the colonel on certain matters," Matt said amiably, as his host handed him a glass of brandy.

"It would be a hell of a life out here if I did," said Forsyth.

They chatted in general for some moments, and finally Forsyth offered another drink.

"That's your third excellent idea, Ned," Matt said with a grin.

Forsyth was holding up his glass, examining the amber fluid as the light from the gaslight fell on it.

"Just what are you really doing out here at Stambaugh, Lieutenant Kincaid?" he asked suddenly.

five _____

Kincaid took his time answering Forsyth's question. He had realized that his story of hunting a renegade Sioux was weak, but it had been the best at hand. What really concerned him, however, was what Blue might be thinking.

"Does the colonel suspect me of some devious motive too?" he asked, parrying Forsyth's question with another.

"I don't know." Forsyth fondled his glass. "He is so conceited, I doubt it would occur to him that someone might try running a sandy on him." He suddenly put his glass down on the table beside him. "Matt, this is all between us. Agreed?"

"Agreed."

"It is the whiskey trains, right?"

"Ned, I'm here looking for those Indians."

A sly smiled licked across the adjutant's face. He was a tall, ruddy-faced man with tight red hair and a neat mustache, and even when relaxing as he was doing now, he seemed to swagger. "You're under orders," he said, as though it were an accusation.

"But of course."

Forsyth sighed. "So we'll leave it at that. I want you to know that I've done all I could to persuade Blue into the more reasonable path; but he's a man with a goddamn mission."

Matt grinned. "That is most certainly evident. I understand he's arrested some men."

"He's going to get us all in a jam if he doesn't watch it. There's money in liquor, and where there's money, there is influence. This whole thing could start a sweet little stampede."

Matt reached for his drink, feeling Forsyth's eyes on him.

"I should warn you, Matt, about one or two things. First of all, I don't believe for a minute that you're after Indians, but we'll let that pass for the moment. I'm going to try to get Blue to invite you to stay over at Stambaugh. You can spend at least two or three days scouting the area without suspicion. If anything will help this stupid situation, I'm for it."

"And is there something else I should be warned about?"

Forsyth's light blue eyes glittered; his grin was

wicked as he surveyed his guest. "Miss Cynthia Blue is, uh, spoken for."

Matt grinned easily. "Good to know."

Forsyth's eyes never moved from Kincaid's face. "It's good that you know it's good to know." And then he let it all burst out in a laugh. "One more for the night, Matt." And he reached for the bottle.

Walking to the guest quarters, where a room had been assigned him, Matt breathed the cool night air deep into his body. His head was clear, and he had thoroughly enjoyed the evening. His thoughts, as he entered his room, were on the girl with the big brown eyes and cornsilk hair. She was really special, and she had definitely been flirting with him, which was of course what provoked Forsyth to speak as he had. But to hell with Forsyth; the girl was too attractive, too provocative to just forget about. At the same time, he knew he mustn't be foolish. He was here on business, not pleasure. The thought sobered him considerably, and while it pained him to realize he had to let go of any pursuit of Cynthia Blue, he knew he had made the right decision.

He had been in bed only a few minutes, somehow not able to drop off to sleep, when he heard something at the door. A pack rat? It sounded now like a tapping. He sat up, leaning on an elbow. It was a knock. Rising swiftly, he crossed the room.

"Who is it?" he asked, speaking low in case the guard was nearby on his rounds.

The voice on the other side of the door was indistinct, yet he was sure it was a woman. With his heart pounding, Matt opened the door and the huddled figure, wrapped in a cape with a large hood, stepped swiftly into the room. The moon, which had been lighting the windowsill, was suddenly hidden by a cloud, and the room became almost totally dark.

The next thing he knew, they were embracing. He had gone to bed in his long underwear, as he usually did; and now, as his hands swept back the girl's cape, her fingers began pulling at his clothing.

In a moment they were naked, lying on the bed, their arms and legs entwined. He entered her easily, for she was soaking wet. Together they rode in a perfect rhythm, as she moaned her exquisite pleasure in his ear, finally exploding in a glorious climax.

They lay gasping, still locked in their embrace. Matt could not believe his great fortune.

And again he grew rigid and now drove his manhood hard into her, as far as he could go. Her body beneath him was firm, resilient, exquisitely active and gentle, demanding and receiving all at once.

Their final consummation blanked him out. It was several moments before he could stir even his thoughts.

"God, you're beautiful," he whispered, as she caressed the side of his face.

"You can't see me," she whispered back. "It's pitch black in here."

"You are beautiful," he insisted.

The girl said nothing. But when he kissed her cheek he tasted the tears.

"Something the matter?" he said softly. "Are you all right?"

"Nothing. Nothing's the matter. I am so happy. Thank you. I thank you." Her lips melted into his. "I have to go now."

It was still dark in the room as she stood up and began dressing. Suddenly the moon came from behind the clouds, and its light spilled into the room. She had her back to him; her body, with its smooth, supple, perfectly proportioned lines, shone like marble.

"You know, you really are beautiful," he said again.

She had pulled on her cape and the hood now, and started toward the door.

"Aren't you going to say goodbye?" he asked, getting up quickly and crossing to her.

They held each other then, her head resting on his chest, and he listened to her sobbing. It lasted only a moment and she had control of herself again.

"Goodnight, sweet prince." Her words were almost inaudible.

"Goodnight, Cynthia."

He had opened the door as he said the words, and she stood on the threshold and half turned to him. He couldn't see her face, because of her hood.

For a moment she stood very still. He could hear her breathing. "Not Cynthia," she said softly. "I am Hester."

And she was gone.

• • •

The day had broken hard and clear over the High Plains. By afternoon it had gotten considerably hotter, the air shimmering above the dry ground.

"Shit, summer's here already," Malone observed, wiping his forehead with his thick forearm and then shaking off the sweat in an elaborate gesture.

Wolfgang Holzer leaned on his double-bitted ax, crossing one foot over the other, looking very casual as he did so. "It is hot, *nicht wahr?* Very vucking hot!"

"Wolfie, you look like a fucking general reviewing the troops," said Private Coy Flanagan, a youth with a luxuriant head of red hair and a mass of freckles all over his innocent-looking face.

Wolfie stepped right into the comic skit by lounging even more languidly, pretending to place a monocle in his eye while inspecting the imaginary soldiers parading before him.

"You want to be one of them German Junkers," Malone said, his Irish accent coming down hard on the *J*, "you better snap to attention."

Instantly, Holzer uncoiled his feet and stood as rigid as a sword, his chest puffed out, his eyes glaring straight ahead while he brought up a slow, majestic salute.

"C'mon, you assholes, get your butts moving!" the gruff voice barked from the other end of the clearing. "You think this wood detail is a goddamn tea party?"

"Sarge, it gets hot here swinging this ax," Malone protested, looking over at Sergeant Bogavich, who was in charge of the detail.

Bogavich, a short, square man with an unlighted

cigar clamped in his jaws, glared back at the big Irishman. This didn't bother Malone at all. He'd had more important people glare at him—notably First Sergeant Ben Cohen—and so he nodded casually and lifted his ax.

"Move it!" Bogavich snarled.

"Yessir, Sergeant Bogavich."

"Malone, cut that 'sir' shit!"

Pursing his lips, his eyelids halfway lowered, Malone brought his ax to his shoulder and turned his back on the sergeant, submitting under elaborate protest to the three stripes on Bogavich's arm.

Wood detail was one of those jobs that came with tedious regularity in the life of the Army of the West. Wood meant firewood, for cooking and for keeping warm during the long winter months. It wasn't necessarily an unpleasant detail, if a man liked physical exercise. Many men did not. This worked to the advantage of Easy Company's first sergeant, who assigned men to the detail at times for punitive reasons. Moreover, wood detail was a good spot for trying out a new recruit. Quickly enough, the hard physical work revealed any disinclination toward labor on the part of a new man.

With Private Tom Tooth, however, it had become immediately apparent that here was a man who did not shirk hard work. And yet, Tooth was not young. Neither was he a sturdy physical specimen. He couldn't weigh more than a hundred and twenty-five, Ben Cohen had thought when he first assigned him to his duties. Yet the elderly recruit worked harder than many men a good deal younger, and at whatever detail he was given. The men liked him, though he seldom spoke. In the evenings he smoked his pipe, and he had even been seen reading a book once or twice. It never occurred to anyone to take advantage of him, even though he was not at all aggressive.

The present wood detail consisted of six men: four woodchoppers and two men standing guard, one of whom was Bogavich, the other of whom was Pop Fegan. The wood party was working in a new stand of trees, for the grove that had been providing the company's fuel had finally been cleared out. A couple of the old hands at wood detail remarked on their pleasure at working in a new and unfamiliar area.

Malone and Holzer were using the axes, while Flanagan and Tooth were teamed up on the crosscut saw. The youngster had removed his hat, and his brilliant red hair shone under the hot sun. He was sweating heavily, and the sight of his soaking shirt and luminous red hair drew friendly laughter from his brother Irishman, Malone.

"That head of hair shine at night, does it, Flanagan?" Malone asked.

Tom Tooth looked down the saw at his partner and smiled. "You know," he said suddenly, "they have places back East where they *buy* hair like that."

Flanagan, who was large and bony, chuckled. "What do they do with it?"

"I don't mean men's hair—and no offense," Tooth added quickly, "but women's long hair."

"You hear that, Flanagan?" said Malone with a loud laugh. "You could maybe sell yours."

"But what do they use it for?" Flanagan asked, his mouth round with surprise. "Not that I'd ever sell it."

"It's a fine head of hair," said Tom Tooth. "I don't know; I only heard it..."

He had barely said those words when the Sioux came screaming out of a small ravine that no one had even noticed was there. The first thing Bogavich felt was the blow that knocked him sprawling. He went flat on his face, the breath knocked out of him having been struck in the back with a thrown tomahawk. Instantly a half dozen hostiles were grappling hand-to-hand with the soldiers. Bogavich, rising to his knees, was just in time to receive the full force of a diving warrior who, knife in hand, was about to scalp him, having already counted coup. Malone found himself locked in combat with a wiry brave who narrowly missed his head with a swinging stone hatchet. Holzer was down on his back, a Sioux on top of him, but just then Flanagan smashed the barrel of his Springfield into the back of the Sioux and then shot him dead. Pop Fegan was creased with a bullet and was now locked in mortal struggle with a warrior who seemed to be totally covered with paint.

Flanagan, after shooting the hostile who had attacked Holzer, was himself driven to his knees by a heavyset warrior who kicked him in the groin and scored his knife along the youth's jaw. Tooth, meanwhile, was borne to the ground by a warrior gripping his windpipe. But the game former Pony Express rider drove his thumbs into his opponent's eyes until the Indian's fingers loosened. Gasping for air, he pushed himself away as the Sioux rolled in agony on the ground. Grabbing up a heavy maul, Tooth smashed it into the warrior's back.

By now the men of Easy Company had rallied from their surprise and were firing their Springfields. Two of the weapons were jammed, and there was no chance for reloading anyway. But they had their six-shooters, and these served to turn the flow of battle.

In a moment the attackers were gone. One Sioux lay dead, killed by Coy Flanagan. Sergeant Bogavich had been creased with a knife along his ribcage, a painful wound, but not serious; and his back was sore, though he'd received no actual wound from that first thrown tomahawk. Flanagan, lying face down in a pool of blood, appeared to be dead.

"Christ, he's been scalped," Malone said, his voice tight with horror and fury.

"Those fuckers!"

"Ve get them!" Holzer said. "Ve go catch them!"

"Don't be an asshole!" Bogavich snarled. "They'll ambush us!"

"He's alive!" Pop Fegan was kneeling beside Flanagan as the fallen man let out a groan of pain. "Coy, are you all right, boy?" Pop asked.

Flanagan gave no sign that he had heard.

"Vat is dis!" cried Wolfgang Holzer. He had moved to the edge of the clearing to be sick, and now, his face as white as paste, he ran toward the group around

Flanagan. He was holding something in his hand.

"What you got there, a fuckin' rat?" Malone bellowed in disgust as Wolfie shoved the wet object in front of the Irishman's face.

"It's a scalp!" declared Bogavich, his big eyes bulging in disbelief. "The buggers dropped it! Christ, it's Flanagan's!"

"They must of dropped his scalp!" Pop Fegan repeated in awe, as the group stood staring at the piece of red hair and flayed skin that Holzer was now delicately holding.

At this point, to everyone's great astonishment, Tom Tooth stepped into the group and, kneeling beside Flanagan, began examining his skull which was a mass of blood. The unfortunate Coy was regaining consciousness, and his cries of agony shook the party of woodcutters.

"Get that bucket of water from under the wagon," Tooth said, and the authority in his voice was unmistakable. No one had ever heard him speak like that before. But someone instantly fetched the bucket. Taking the scalp out of Holzer's hand, Tooth dropped it into the water.

"It'll maybe keep it fresh till we get back to the post. Get him into the wagon—but gently," Tooth said. "Be real gentle with him. Put those blankets under him."

"What the hell are you doing, Tooth?" Bogavich demanded, suddenly confronting this new authority standing before him.

"Trying to save his hair for him, Sergeant—and his

59

life. Can we get back to the post fast?"

"I wasn't thinkin' of doing anything else, for Christ's sake," replied Bogavich. "Load up! Let's go!"

As the horse and wagon, driven by Pop Fegan, raced back to Number Nine, the sergeant stared at Pony Tom Tooth.

"What the hell you saving that hairpiece for?" he asked.

"Might get it back on him," Tooth said. "That's too good a head of hair to lose like that. Coy really admired his red hair."

"Seems the Sioux did too," Bogavich said, clamping his teeth on his cigar butt.

Flanagan was writhing in agony at every lurch of the wagon, while Pony Tom held the boy's bloody head in his lap in an effort to ease the brutal ride.

"You thinking Rothausen can sew that scalp back on?" Bogavich's big eyes stared at Tooth. "Hell, Dutch is our acting sawbones all right, but Jesus, he's still only a mess sergeant, a fucking butcher! I sure wouldn't want him carving me."

"No," Tooth said calmly, looking off into the sky. "Neither would I."

"I never heard of a scalp being sewed back on."

"It's worth a try," Tooth said. "But we have to act fast."

"We?" Bogavich repeated. "Who you figure will sew that thing back on him?"

Pony Tom turned his calm gray eyes directly on Sergeant Bogavich. "I'd like to give it a try, Sarge. With your permission."

Bogavich stared at Private Tooth. The unlighted cigar butt fell to the floor of the swaying wagon box.

Tom Tooth realized suddenly that the cigar must have stayed clamped in the sergeant's jaws during the whole of the Indian attack.

six ─────────────────────

Fast and high the game had opened, so that the betting was crisp, and the three whiskey-train prisoners had little time to worry over their fate.

They were being held in a section of barracks, under guard, and were allowed out only for exercise. They had their own deck of cards, a torn, greasy pack that looked as old and battered as the men themselves. They were playing for splinters, as they called it, using slivers of wood they picked off the fire logs by the potbellied stove. To ease the pain and boredom, they had a further resource. The three men had had the presence of mind to act swiftly under the holocaust that Blue had unleashed; thus they had managed to smuggle in a few bottles of good, honest whiskey. Besides this support, the irrational conduct of Colonel Blue and his soldiers had not extended to Doc Lightfoot's Sure-Shot Panacea; the whole of Doc's supply had gone unscathed, Doc's very body protecting the case containing "the medicinal miracle of the century" from the depradations of the vandals. Such histrionics and swift footwork had always been Clarence Lightfoot's strong points.

Thus, the trio was presently enjoying a happy social occasion, sipping whiskey and patent medicine. Doc had suggested mixing the two, in view of the fact that they were longer on Panacea than on whiskey. All agreed it was a joyful concoction.

For a good while now, Doc had won every pot. Barney Smith laughed, joked, told racy stories. Herkimer Bill, still dreaming of his comeback on the outlaw trail, discovered that he was almost wiped out of splinters, then suddenly found that he had three aces over Doc's three kings and Barney's tens, and he raked in a big pot.

Two hands later, Barney dragged in a sizeable pot, and the game began to even out.

In the next hand, Herkimer Bill Fall drew one card and opened the bidding with a hundred dollars in splinter money. But Doc Lightfoot found that fortune had decorated his hand with three deuces.

"Raise you a hundred," he said, advancing a stack of splinters.

Each reached for the bottle, Herkimer Bill getting there first, and almost knocking it over.

"For Christ's sake, careful there!" cried Doc.

Herkimer chuckled. "Didn't do it," he said. "Tried to, by damn, and I didn't do 'er."

"And I up you," Barney Smith said.

The betting shuttled back and forth until the pot of splinters stood at close to four thousand imaginary dollars. Doc's eyes were bugging out of his head. Barney and Herkimer Bill were sweating heavily.

Doc, praising heaven as he reached for a card, found his prayers answered. He held a fourth deuce.

"Gentlemen, I call. What have you got?"

Barney Smith whistled out a laugh and fanned his cards dramatically across the upturned crate that was their table. "Three tens."

"Hah!" snorted Herkimer Bill. "Have a look—three fat queens, the way I like 'em, and a pair of fours!"

A pause fell into the game. Barney and Bill finally looked over at Doc Lightfoot. Doc's face showed no expression as he laid down his four deuces.

"Glory be, he has spoked the pair of us," announced Herkimer Bill. "You slickered us, goddamn ya!"

"Tinhorn!" snarled Barney Smith.

But before the moment could develop more heat, they heard the key turn in the lock of the door to their quarters. Instantly the bottles were swept from sight and the game resumed, the players wrapped in quiet and innocence as the guard preceded Colonel Blue and Captain Forsyth into the room. The party was followed by a tall, bulging man in greasy buckskins, wearing a fur cap, a pair of skinning knives, a big Navy Colt, and very long hair that hung down to his shoulders.

A strong smell of bear grease accompanied the party, and it was assumed by the three whiskey-train prisoners to come from the individual in buckskin. They were correct. The miscreants soon discovered that they were in the company of one of the most famous scouts of the Wyoming Territory, Sweetwater John Johnson.

"I heard of him," Barney Smith whispered swiftly to Herkimer Bill, his elixir-soaked breath wiping out the smell of bear grease. "What'n hell's he messin' with this army feller for? He drinks more whiskey in a day than a fucking buffalo takes water in August."

"I expect you men have not been uncomfortable here," the colonel said, frowning at the greasy deck of cards spread over the crate. "However, I am certain that you would wish to cooperate with the army so that there might arise the possibility of, shall we say, mitigation of the charges against you."

"What's he sayin'?" asked Barney Smith, squinting at the two officers and the scout, then cocking his head toward Doc and Herkimer Bill.

"Shit, Barney, you got so much hair sproutin' out of yer ears, it's a wonder you can hear anything." Herkimer Bill rumbled out a little laugh at this.

"Well, sir, Colonel, sir, what can we do for you?" Doc addressed the visitors in his most engaging manner. "Eh? That's the question. Ah—hah! The captor has come to the captive. Not on bended knee! Ah, no! But he has come!" And Doc's face parted in a great reddish grin as the tip of his tongue showed between his gray whiskers.

"What's he saying?" insisted Barney, as the colonel outlined what he wanted.

"He is saying," Herkimer Bill explained, "that if we show him where the whiskey is coming from and who the whiskey seller is, and where the whiskey is going to, and who will buy it, he might give us a extra piece of cake for supper." Herkimer Bill kept his eyes cold on the colonel as he spoke, and now they glinted as they saw the frown sweeping into Blue's tense face.

"I have told you what you can do to serve the cause of law and order," the colonel snapped.

"Tell him no," Herkimer said as Doc took a step forward, ready to speak.

"We will think it over, sir, Colonel Blue," Doc Lightfoot said. "We do not see that we done anything wrong. Fact is, we didn't. But we will turn it over, study it, if you won't mind giving us a bit of time." Doc spoke long-windedly, as he always did, and with a dignity that matched the colonel's.

"You have twenty-four hours," snapped Colonel Blue, and he turned and strode from the room, almost ramming into the sentry, who had to dive out of his way.

A grin started to break out on Sweetwater John's face, but he killed it. Instead, scowling at the trio, he said, "Better do what he wants. He is not fooling around when it comes to busting up whiskey."

"Sweetwater, what the hell you doing with a jasper like that?" Barney Smith asked.

"Man's got to protect his own interests," Sweetwater John Johnson said as he strode through the door after Blue and his adjutant. But none of the three missed the wink he dropped as he said those words.

Several hours and much conversation and liquor later, they decided they would do as the colonel requested.

"He has got us by the balls, no matter how you slice it," Barney Smith observed sagely.

Herkimer Bill's long tongue licked out between the hair around his aged, cracked lips.

"We got to do like he says, 'pears to me," he said.

"It'll be Jake who cuts our balls off," observed Doc. "We are getting it up the old rooty-tooty, coming and going!" And the old boy wiggled his behind to the delight of his companions, who fell into a fit of coughing laughter.

"What the hell we gonna do?"

"Tell him no."

"Then he'll really ream us."

"Tell him we'll do it."

"Then Jake'll jump up our ass. We ain't gettin' paid to haul this whiskey so the fuckin' prairie can drink it!"

"I got it," Doc said suddenly. In the silence that followed this dramatic utterance, he reached for his drink of whiskey and Sure-Shot Panacea.

"We will go along with the colonel," Doc said, speaking each word slowly.

"That is plumb crazy!" said Herkimer Bill, scratching his behind furiously.

"But we will only pretend to go along with it."

"Aha!" Barney Smith's eyes gleamed. "Good thinking there." He took a step forward, a bit unsteady on his feet. "Good thinking, old friend."

"Genius inevitably will out," Doc declared. "We will pretend. Meanwhile, we'll get off another message to Barney's sutler friend that we are in dire trouble. And—"

"And at the same time we can look to find ways to excape the hell outta here!" Herkimer Bill cried joyously. "By God, boys, that calls for a drink!"

"I want to know what makes you think you can sew that scalp back on Flanagan's head, soldier." The first sergeant of Easy Company was staring incredulously at Private Tom Tooth as he said those words.

"Sergeant, if it isn't done pretty fast, he won't have much chance of having his hair sewed back on at all."

"I want an answer to my question."

"I don't know, Sarge. I've seen it done. Why not give it a try, was what I asked myself when Holzer came running up with that scalp in his hand."

There was definitely something in Tooth's bearing that deflected any rebuttal Cohen might have made. The first sergeant was a sensitive man. He felt the change in Tooth, heard the affirmation of something in his tone of voice, smelled it coming from him. The private standing before him was not the Pony Tom Tooth they had known. Definitely. The man was small, but he was solid. He stood his ground. He knew what he was up to. This was no bullshit, Ben Cohen could see that clearly. He liked that. He liked it, but he didn't say so.

He said, "I will speak to the captain."

"We have got to work fast, Sergeant. Flanagan is in a lot of pain."

"I been able to figure that out, soldier," Ben Cohen said, sour as vinegar.

Tom Tooth wisely kept his mouth shut. At this point, Captain Conway walked into the orderly room.

"What's this I hear about one of the men being scalped, Ben?"

"It's Flanagan, sir. Second Platoon. Tooth here claims he can sew his scalp back on."

Conway turned his eyes fully upon Pony Tom Tooth, sizing him up with a swift, penetrating look.

"How?"

"Captain, I have seen it done. I think I can do it."

Conway kept his eyes squarely on Tooth, measuring him for falsity, intelligence, maybe even madness.

"What do you think, Ben?"

"It's a chance, sir. I somehow feel like trying it. For sure, Rothausen can't help him, and Flanagan's in bad shape. He's lost a lot of blood. It's a miracle he's still alive. And it was Tooth here who helped him, riding back in the wood wagon. He seems to know what he's doing."

"You're saying we've got nothing to lose."

"Yes, sir, that's about the size of it."

A second or two passed. Conway nodded. "Give him whatever he needs, Sergeant." Turning back to

70

Tooth, he said, "Good luck, soldier."

"Thank you, sir."

Conway started toward his office. "I want to see Flanagan. Where is he, Sergeant?"

"In the room next to the mess hall, sir."

"Tell Rothausen and anyone else available to give this soldier whatever help he needs."

And Warner Conway closed his office door behind him. He stood for a moment in the quiet room, looking over at the window, but standing very still. *My God,* he was thinking, *this is a crazy army.*

In the room next to the enlisted mess, Tooth stood looking down at Coy Flanagan, who was stretched out on a table.

"I want a lot of clean sheets and bandages," he said. "And blankets. I want his head raised, and someone—you"—he nodded to Malone—"hold his head, like this." He took Flanagan's head gently in his hands and showed what he meant.

Malone, with no color at all in his face, stepped over and took hold of Flanagan. "We're with you, boy," he muttered.

"Bring hot water," Tooth said. "Somebody go to the barracks. Fast! I've got a sack in my duffel there. Bring it. Run!"

He had stepped back from the table and was rolling up his sleeves.

"If you're going to sew him," Bogavich said, "won't you need a needle and thread? Dutch Rothausen has that stuff."

"That's just what I sent for," Tooth replied.

71

Dutch Rothausen, mess sergeant and Easy Company's acting medic, stared bug-eyed at the scene before him. But the attitude of Ben Cohen, and the others present silenced him.

When the captain entered the room with Lieutenants Taylor and Fitzgerald, Tooth was busily at work. Flanagan, loaded with whiskey from Conway's private supply, had mercifully passed out.

"Never heard of a scalp getting *onto* somebody's head," the awed Dutch Rothausen whispered to Windy Mandalian in the silence that gripped the room.

Windy said nothing. All eyes were on Tooth, all faces set in fascination as the hands of the former Pony Express rider flew at their task. Tooth knew exactly what he was doing. He worked quickly, but he did not hurry.

When he was through, he stepped back from the table, his face soaked with sweat, his bloody hands at his sides. "We should keep him here," he said. "Don't move him. Two men better stay with him to see that he doesn't roll off the table."

Flanagan was still out, but his scalp of bright red hair was back on his head.

"That is a real nice head of red hair," Windy said softly. "It would've been a shame to lose it."

"He is not going to lose it," Pony Tom Tooth said.

"Jesus!" Sergeant Bogavich turned to Ben Cohen. "Now we know how the Pony Express made it through."

Tom Tooth was standing very still. He was very white in the face as he walked over to a bucket of water standing beside the one that had carried Flanagan's scalp, and began to wash his hands and arms.

Conway said, "Sergeant Cohen, see that Private Tooth has whatever he needs." And he nodded toward the bottle of whiskey that had allayed the agony of Coy Flanagan.

"Yes, sir."

Warner Conway walked over to Tooth, who was drying his hands. "Good work, soldier."

"Thank you, sir." The smile that flitted onto Tom Tooth's face was wan. "I believe he'll pull through."

Conway snorted as he turned to the room. "Of course he'll pull through. He's a redheaded, red-freckled Irishman."

It was what was needed. The men were joking and laughing, though quietly, as they left the room.

Ben Cohen was the last to leave, save for Tooth and the two men watching Flanagan. Handing the bottle to Tooth, he said, "Put that where it'll do the most good. Captain's orders, soldier."

The grin that now appeared on Tom Tooth's face was sunny. "Would it be out of line to ask the first sergeant to join me?"

Ben Cohen stopped in his tracks and turned. His eyes opened wide as he surveyed the man before him.

"The first sergeant will be happy to accept your invitation, Private Tooth. But it'll be better done in the orderly room than here. We don't want to lead anyone into temptation," he said, throwing a glance at Flanagan's companions.

Sometime later in the day, after the bottle had been well addressed, and as Ben Cohen and Tooth were crossing the parade, the first sergeant said, "Tell me, Tooth, what do you recommend for corns? I'm getting a hell of a corn on my big toe, and I'm telling you, I can't get rid of it."

seven _____

The following morning, Private Tooth stood at attention in front of the desk of his commanding officer.

"At ease, soldier." Conway studied the man before him for a long moment, then moved his eyes to Ben Cohen, who was standing nearby. Finally he returned his full attention to Tooth.

"I watched you working on Flanagan, soldier. I'd say it wasn't that you'd just seen an operation like that, as you told me. I'd suggest you'd done it before." He paused. "Or at any rate, something similar."

"Yes, sir."

"Yes, what? You have done it."

"I have never sutured on a scalp, sir, but I have sutured the odd cut now and then."

"You're a doctor?"

"I studied medicine, sir."

"You better tell it straight, soldier." Ben Cohen growled the words, seeing the frown starting on Conway's face.

"Yes, Sergeant." Tooth turned back to Conway. "Sir, I was a medical student."

"What happened?"

"Sir, I—lost my chance to ever practice medicine."

"I'd like to know why."

"Captain . . ." For the first time, Tooth was clearly having trouble. His eyes dropped away from Conway's face. But then he rallied and now stood firmly looking at his commanding officer.

"Sir, with all due respect . . . must I?"

Conway swept his eyes to Ben Cohen, then back to Tooth. "I need to know, soldier, but maybe not just at this particular moment. Think it over. For the present, I will say that you performed above and beyond the call of duty. Perhaps for now we'll just let sleeping dogs lie." He leaned slightly forward. "For the moment," he added.

"Thank you, sir. I am very grateful."

"Will Flanagan pull through all right?"

"He's going to be all right, sir. He'll have a bad headache for a while, that's all."

"We all have that," Ben Cohen observed.

Conway looked directly at Tooth. "Private Tooth, I just want it to be clear. If there is anything connected with the law, anything that might involve Easy Company, you'd better tell me right now."

"It's nothing to do with the law, sir. It's all done, all in the past."

"You were an Express rider?"

"Yes, sir. But this was something to do with my medical career. A patient... a patient died."

"I see."

"I joined the army to start over, Captain."

Conway leaned back a little. "I understand, soldier." He paused, his eyes looking at a spot on Tooth's chin. "Very well, then. Dismissed."

When the door had closed behind Pony Tom Tooth, Conway turned to his first sergeant. "Well, Ben?"

"He's a good soldier, sir. I mean, apart from what he did for Flanagan. He works hard, keeps his nose clean."

"You think he's on the square with us?"

"Yes, sir. I think Tooth is square."

Conway stood up. "He says it's all past history. I just hope that anyone who was involved in whatever happened with Tooth also considers it past history."

Ben Cohen's mouth opened, but he said nothing, only nodding his head very slowly. Then he said, "I never thought of that, sir."

"I did. The question is, Sergeant Cohen, did Tooth join the army really to start his life over? Or was he thinking it was a good place to hide?"

"Each man has his own weakness," the colonel was saying as he strode back and forth in his office. He was carrying his gauntlets in his left hand, and these he slapped against his thigh at certain points during the conversation. "It's the sure way to know him." He paused and slapped at his thigh. "To know the man's weakness is to know the man," he intoned. It was his habit to repeat himself whenever he felt that what he'd said was especially good. The colonel, Matt noted, dealt in quotes.

Sweetwater John Johnson leaned against the door-jamb, his arms folded on his big chest, one leg crossed over the other, his head cocked to one side as he chewed, sniffed, and looked from beneath lowered lids at Colonel Jonathan Blue.

It was mostly to Matt Kincaid that Blue was addressing himself. Matt was seated in a straight-backed wooden chair in front of the colonel's mahogany desk. Blue's straight, high-backed black leather chair seemed, even without him sitting in it, to emphasize his presence. Matt felt he could have spoken to the chair, it was so like its owner.

However, the colonel was warming up on his office promenade. He did his best thinking while in movement. His voice was sharp, the words clear and quick from the tight lips, as he outlined his philosophy and plan for the extinction of whiskey trains in the Wyoming Territory.

"It is the devil's swill," he had declared at the beginning of his monologue. From that position he had fanned out to other dissipations such as tobacco, gambling, and women.

"No question that physical release with a woman is

necessary, Kincaid. No question. But it is too often taken to excess. Men become beasts, swinish in their carnality. I've seen it, Lieutenant. Oh, I have seen it!" He wagged his tight little head, with his black hair plastered to it like patent leather. "Of course, it is the whiskey and other of those waters that encourage the debauchery!"

He slapped his thigh, turned at the far end of the room, and stood still, his forefinger raised as he faced Kincaid and Sweetwater John. "The mind sleeps, and the body's lusts spring forth!"

"Good quote, sir," said Matt. "Where is that from, Colonel?"

A smile creased Blue's face. "It is from the unpublished work of, uh, Jonathan Blue, Lieutenant."

Matt laughed with surprise. "It's really good. I mean that. I had no idea you were such a literary man, Colonel."

Blue's eyes broadened into pure delight. His shoulders, already at attention, moved even further back as he raised himself up on his toes, and then came down. His lips pursed, his eyebrows lifted in modest diffidence. There was a meaningful gleam in his eyes as he said, "I dabble. Someday I shall commit certain things to paper. Hmm. Certain things," he repeated. "For what is worth saying once is worth saying twice, don't you know."

He resumed his pacing, while Matt followed him with his eyes. His thoughts however, were on the problem confronting him. No small matter, yet he had discovered to his surprise that Blue was only too glad to share his ideas and plans on his whiskey crusade. "A man saved from John Barleycorn is an ally in the Great Crusade," he had put it, simply assuming that Kincaid was a man who had defeated the bottle.

Not having even a vague idea of how to go about his mission, Matt had simply thought the best thing was to get close to the colonel and see what turned up. It had all happened beautifully. He was finding himself accepted as a potential crusader. The remarkable thing was that Blue didn't appear to have an inkling of any problem that he might be creating in the army, or even that he was acting out of order. Yet, for Matt, there still remained the question of how he was going to cut down the zealous colonel without the backing of higher authority. At this point, all he could think of was how much he needed a drink.

"I do think it's a good idea to release the prisoners, though, Colonel," Matt said suddenly, returning to an earlier part of the long monologue.

"A good idea, you say? Only because I have had the intelligence to understand their motives. Unquestionably, the recalcitrants should be punished. There is no question that punishment should be their portion," he repeated. "Punishment for their sins against the holy temple of the body, not to mention the soul," he added, his voice dropping as he stood before a wall map of Wyoming Territory.

"But you see, Kincaid, there is bigger game than that wanton trio. I shall release them. I have offered them their freedom—which they will, without doubt, instantly turn into license—on condition that they lead us to their source of supply. That is to say, lead us to the person or persons who profit most from this wretched enterprise which has corrupted not only the honorable soldier but the miserable redskin."

"And they agreed, did they?" Matt asked. He was finding it difficult to keep the right pitch of interest in his voice, for he had been listening for a full hour to the colonel.

The colonel came to a halt. "They have had the unmitigated temerity to say that they want to think over my offer—if you please!" He brought his heavy gauntlets down smartly on his thigh.

Sweetwater John, his eyes hooded with boredom close to actual sleep, wondered if by now that thigh wasn't bruised.

Raising and lowering himself on his toes, Blue let his words sink in, fully expecting his listeners to be as outraged as he was himself. He was an incredibly short man, Matt realized. He could hardly restrain a grin as he thought of the three whiskey-train oldsters with their sowbelly talk and ruminations, their inhuman odor, and their sly wit, defying the whippy little Blue, who seemed to be getting enmeshed in their indolence as surely as a fly in a glue pot. If the colonel wasn't careful, Matt told himself, his impatience would get him in trouble not only with those three slickers, but with the whole whiskey-train drama.

At this point, Sweetwater John eased himself into the tableau. "Colonel, I'll allow that if you want to succeed in getting them fellers to lead you any-wheres—like to their leader—you better go about it different."

"How so? What do you mean, different? Speak up, man! Can't hear a word when you mumble!"

Sweetwater John wasn't even looking at the commanding officer of Fort Stambaugh. He was looking for the cuspidor.

Matt pointed toward a corner of the room. Sweet-water ambled over, spat heavily, and returned to the doorjamb.

"Well?" Blue was almost dancing with impatience.

"Well what, Colonel, sir?" Sweetwater's mouth opened in a big circle with the tip of his tongue protruding, as his forehead wrinkled and he blinked his eyes very fast.

"Stop that idiotic clowning, man!" snapped Blue furiously.

A grin spread slowly, all the way across Sweetwater John's face. "Just trying to get your attention, Colonel," he said, and winked at Kincaid.

"How do you think I should go about it differently?"

"I am saying, Colonel, that if you want success with that caper, you better fix it so's them fellers think they have excaped."

Jonathan Blue hesitated for just an instant. "And follow them to their leader, eh?" he said, his enthusiasm obviously having been whetted. "But of course, man. You must have been reading my thoughts. I'd been about to say just that. In fact, I was on the point of ordering my first sergeant to make such arrangements." He strode the length of the room, which was not very long, slapping his gauntlets against his hard little leg.

"It will have to be done carefully, Johnson. It must not be bungled! Damn it, Johnson, if anyone bungles it, I will have him court-martialed!"

"Custer had 'em spread-eagled on a wagon wheel, Colonel," Sweetwater John said, speaking slowly around his chew.

"For desertion, my man. For deserting the army. A capital offense!" He paused, standing still in the middle of the room. "Still, an example might be set. But of course, only if necessary. Only if necessary."

"Sounds like a good idea to me, Colonel," Matt said agreeably. "I mean, letting them escape," he added quickly.

The colonel shot a glance, as sharp as a bird's, at Sweetwater John Johnson. "On second thought, I think you should make the arrangements for the—er—escape. Such derring-do, I do believe, is more in your line of work than in mine. We are less covert in the army, Johnson. More open and on the up-and-up."

"I do bet you are, Colonel," Sweetwater John said as he opened the door and ambled out, belching softly.

It was a major plan, Colonel Jonathan Blue was thinking—a favorite phrase of his—as he walked out of his office an hour later and headed toward his quarters. He was about halfway there when Captain Forsyth came walking fast across the parade.

"Sir, a word with you..."

"But of course, Captain. What is it?"

"Sir, I understand from Johnson that you were planning on releasing the prisoners if they would reveal who their boss is; and that you then changed that to a different plan."

"Allowing them to escape," the colonel interrupted testily. "What's the matter?"

"They *have* escaped, sir."

"Well, that was the plan, was it not, Captain?"

"Yes, sir. So it was. The only thing is, the prisoners had already escaped by the time we got round to *letting* them escape."

"You mean they escaped anyway? Is that what you are telling me, Captain Forsyth?"

"Sir..."

At this point, the colonel exploded.

"I'll have their balls, sir! I'll have their balls in a skillet, damn me if I don't!"

eight ━━━━━━━━━━━━━

Using the excuse of looking for the renegade Sioux he'd supposedly been tracking, Matt Kincaid rode out of Fort Stambaugh and headed north. He had decided to follow the three escaped prisoners on his own—leaving Wojensky and Nolan at the fort—to see where they might lead him. Sweetwater John Johnson, meanwhile, had already been dispatched by Jonathan Blue with the same purpose in mind. Matt had waited until the scout was well on his way before leaving the post.

His precaution was useless as it turned out, for he hadn't been away from the fort longer than an hour when a figure on horseback appeared around a cutback just ahead on the trail. It was, of course, Sweetwater John.

"Figured you'd be along, Lieutenant, so thought I'd wait, see if we could join up."

"Glad for the company," Kincaid said. "You see any sign of Sioux?"

"Don't reckon you have, neither," Sweetwater said with a slow grin. "I do see plenty sign of them three whiskey peddlers."

"They have cut quite a swath," Matt said, smiling as they rode side by side along the open trail. "Do you think they'll lead you to their boss?"

Sweetwater John shrugged. "Right now they are leading the both of us to Smith's Town," he said.

It was clear to Kincaid that the scout was well aware of the real purpose of his visit to Stambaugh, and so he decided to drop all pretenses.

"Ever been to Smith's Town, Lieutenant?" Sweetwater asked.

"No, I'm not from around this part of the country, you know."

"I know. But I know you been to Denver on account of you said so, and you ain't from that part of the country, neither."

Matt laughed aloud. "But I'm looking forward to seeing Smith's Town," he said.

The scout chuckled. "Good enough."

"I've heard some things about the place."

"And all is true. All is true."

"Smith's Town is in Smith's Gulch, isn't that right?" Kincaid asked.

Sweetwater John Johnson squinted into the distance. "That is right. That is where it's at," he said. "Just a little bit north and a little bit south of hell."

As a rule the more lively Western towns maintained a division, or deadline—usually the railroad tracks—separating the respectable part of town from that area often referred to as the "cabbage patch." Here the more colorful individuals—gamblers, conmen, transient cowboys, and those rare soldiers who could manage now and again to afford it—cavorted round the clock with liquor, music and dance, cards, and assuredly with those to whom the more pious and straitlaced referred as "soiled doves."

There was no railroad at Smith's Town, nor any deadline. The fact was, the whole town was a cabbage patch, consisting of a dozen or so roughly built wooden houses, two of which were dance halls, and four of which were straight saloons. There was also a hotel—the Boston House—a funeral parlor, a livery, a general store, and two eateries. Besides these, there were four structures that had started to become buildings of some sort or other, but had never been completed. Possibly someone had run out of money or enterprise or both. At any rate, Smith's Town must have realized it wasn't going to grow.

Brown, dusty, and forlorn-looking in the middle of a great dun-colored gash in the prairie—Smith's Gulch—the town was at the butt end of no place at all, as Sweetwater John had put it to Kincaid.

The two dance halls stood close together, with a

patch of yellow-brown, well-trodden grass between them. Jolly's Place was owned and operated by Ace Jolly, the other establishment was known as The Wizard's Good Times Parlor, after its proprietor, Harold the Wizard, who also served as the town undertaker. No one knew how Harold had earned his unique sobriquet, or even if he had a second name; but as some wag had put it, the Wizard was clearly enlarging his life's vocation of dealing with dead bodies in his funeral establishment while occupying himself with live ones at his Good Times Parlor.

A bar was a definite part of each of these lively places of dance and refreshment, and it was mandatory that the dancers patronize it at the conclusion of each set. Drinks cost twenty-five cents each. The bar charged two dollars for a dance. It was no place for the humble soldier with his thirteen-dollars-a-month pay. Mostly, Smith's Town catered to the transients who stopped by on their way to or from the South Pass. It didn't matter which direction the traveler was going, he invariably departed Smith's Town with a good deal less money than he had with him on arrival.

In a back room of Harold the Wizard's Good Times Parlor, a group of earnest poker players were hunched around a baize-topped table while a small collection of hangers-on stood about, watching the play.

The game was jacks or better, and the action was brisk. Among the players were those three whiskey-train operators, who were enjoying their first respite since escaping from Fort Stambaugh, stealing horses from the nearby Tipi Town, and cutting it fast to Smith's

Town. It had been Barney Smith's sutler friend who arranged it, and to him they were now drinking in gratitude, Doc Lightfoot foregoing his Sure-Shot. The liquor proved to be very nearly as good anyway, he'd decided.

The other players consisted of a former stage driver named Frank O'Purse, an ex-miner named Wiley Wiles, a nondescript cowboy, and an extraordinary individual wrapped in a collection of coats, shawls, and beads, and smoking a short, thick, foul-smelling cigar. Through the haze of smoke that hovered like a cloud above the table, there appeared a gray head atop the firmly wrapped garments and cigar, with its hair wrapped in a loose bun, its ears small and close to the head. The face itself revealed a cynical twist to the wide mouth, once the cigar was removed, and a pair of flint-sharp gray eyes that surveyed the other players coldly from across a small hill of chips that attested to the person's skill at cards.

"Jake, I'll see ya," Frank O'Purse was saying, and he shoved forward some chips.

"It's cold as a bitch in here, colder'n a whore's ass on Sunday morning," the cigar-smoking figure replied with no expression at all. The voice was high, raspy, and absolutely definite—not the sort of voice anyone wanted to argue with.

Poker Jake, or Jacqueline Dumfernline, as the lady would have been known on her birth certificate if she'd had one, nodded at O'Purse and pushed a stack of chips forward. "See ya, Frank." Those gray eyes gazed across the table at O'Purse, as cold and hard as stones.

Someone had once said that they looked like the eyes of a snake. Nor did the equanimity of that singular lady change now as she raked in her winnings.

It was Clarence Lightfoot's deal. Accepting the deck, he released a flamboyant sigh of pleasure, and leaning his sharp elbows on the dirty green baize tabletop, he held the deck in one hand and fanned it open at eye level.

Raising his hairy eyebrows, he smiled. "A pack of cards, my friends. Of old, it was known as the devil's prayer book." He chuckled, his blue bandanna bobbing up and down on his Adam's apple.

Expertly he shuffled, cut, dealt. Then he sat back in his chair, lips pursed, brows raised, lids lowered to his cards.

"Rich gamblers and old trumpeters are rare, as the saying has it." Doc folded his hand and placed the cards face down before him.

Poker Jake's face remained impassive. "You are full of shit," she said.

Doc was equal to the moment, barking out a laugh. "Jake, I love ya!"

"Wait'll you're ast, you dirty old fuck, you!"

This brought a brisk round of chortling from the assembly, with Poker Jake abstaining from any expression whatsoever. The players, all of whom were in her employ as drivers and helpers with whiskey trains, were more or less used to her behavior. She paid well, but she also played cards better than any of them had ever encountered before. Most of them would have agreed, if asked, that it was not a vile servitude.

Now the game slowed a little. After a few hands, when Doc had slightly increased his bank and the others had just about held even, Poker Jake reached for a fresh deck.

"Ante a dollar," she said, and clamped her teeth tightly on her cigar.

Nobody objected, and the money was put into the pot.

"Pass," Barney Smith said with a loud sniff.

Poker Jake relighted her cigar, after striking a wooden lucifer one-handed on her thumbnail.

Herkimer Bill opened. "I'll make it a dollar for a starter. And it sure beats playing for splinters."

"Looks like I am in," Doc said, and he took a drink from the glass at his elbow.

Poker Jake simply watched her cards and puffed at her cigar.

Frank O'Purse tossed in a silver cartwheel.

"Dealer stays." Poker Jake kept her eyes low, waiting.

Barney Smith pushed forward a dollar and drew two cards.

A sort of grin appeared on Wiley Wiles' round face. "One card," he said. "And let it be a happy one."

"I will accept three of the pasteboards," Doc said.

He looked at the three cards Poker Jake dealt, and tossed them into the discard. "A man gets no thanks for what he loseth at play." Sniffing, he settled back in his chair, rubbing his belly gently, and smiling at Poker Jake.

"Well," said Herkimer Bill, releasing a gentle belch

into his cards as he examined them. "I oughta pass, but we'll see where the men are—and the boys."

Poker Jake took her cigar out of her mouth to say, "Fuck off! There ain't a man in the whole fuckin' bunch of yez."

Color swept into Herkimer's old face. "Very well. Table stakes? I'll bet five."

Barney Smith pushed five dollars into the pot. "And another five," he said, counting it out in cartwheels.

Herkimer Bill grinned behind his wild beard.

"I pass," said O'Purse.

"And another five," said Herkimer Bill.

The level of Poker Jake's voice was inflexible. "I'll just call."

"I call your five and raise you five more," Barney Smith said.

Herkimer Bill squinted at his cards, which he held tightly in his two hands, curving them slightly. "I will see you and raise you five."

At this point Poker Jake said, "I call, and raise the pot another ten dollars."

Herkimer's mouth dropped open like a little door, while first astonishment and then pique flashed across Barney Smith's countenance.

"Dammit! Shit, falling for that old turkey. Letting the last bet go by. By cracky, I'll bet my ass to a teakettle you got four of a kind!"

"One way to find out." Poker Jake's words turned suddenly into a cough as she sprayed saliva around the table.

"Well, we'll soon see," Barney Smith said grimly. "Herkimer!"

"I'm in. Let's have a look-see." His eyes were wide as he leaned forward.

"Boys, the drinks are on me," Poker Jake said, as she laid down four kings and an ace and raked in the final pot.

Someone rose and turned down the coal-oil lamp. Dawn had come.

The poker players sat in their chairs for a few moments longer. Once again, Poker Jake had wiped them out. But they were not sorry. They'd all had a good time.

It was just as the winner was reaching for her glass of whiskey that the door leading into the main barroom opened and Harold the Wizard walked in. He was wearing his apron and there were dots of perspiration on the top of his totally bald head.

"Couple visitors out in the bar, Jake," he said.

"Lawmen?"

"One a soldier, the other Sweetwater John Johnson. I got a notion they be looking for someone." And the Wizard dropped his pale eyes to Herkimer Bill, Barney Smith, and Clarence Lightfoot.

An appalling silence had gripped the men sitting around the table. All turned their eyes toward Poker Jake.

"The Good Lord has initiated an excruciating move," declared Doc Lightfoot. "We are in your hands, Jake. What do you recommend? The enterprise, as we told you on our arrival, is gravely endangered by this tiny idiot of a colonel, or whatever he is."

Poker Jake took the cigar out of her mouth. "He may be an idiot, that soldier feller," she said. "But the U.S. Army ain't—you dumbbells!" She stared at them, her expressionless face far more terrifying than if she'd exhibited high anger.

"What'll we do?" Herkimer Bill asked.

"Git yer asses out the back door and stay out of sight. I'll talk to them two. But let 'em wait a spell." And she nodded to the Wizard as she calmly reached for her glass of whiskey. After taking a hefty drink, she put the glass down. Then she picked up the cards, arranged them, shuffled, and began dealing herself three-card monte.

nine ————————————

At Outpost Number Nine, a thin, cold rain came slicing down out of a metal-colored sky. The men, dampened physically, and in spirit as well, went about their tasks in desultory fashion. Even the first sergeant's bark seemed muted by the weather. Ben Cohen was by no means out of action, however. He growled over Dutch Rothausen's coffee, swore at an itch he couldn't immediately locate, and snapped at the company clerk, glaring at the message that Four Eyes Bradshaw handed him.

First Sergeant Ben Cohen's glare shortly turned into a look of serious thought as he read again the words that had come over the telegraph from Regiment. Now his eyes went to the door of Captain Warner Conway's office. It was shut, and Ben Cohen had the definite feeling that his commanding officer wanted it kept that way. Easy Company's first sergeant usually respected his own hunches, especially in matters pertaining to his CO. Still, the dispatch from Regiment did require Conway's attention. He hesitated, his eyes dropping again to the paper lying on the desk in front of him, his thoughts working quickly at Easy Company's latest problem. Automatically, Cohen's big, heavy-knuckled hand reached out for his cup of coffee. It wasn't until he put the cup back down on his desk that he realized that though he had finished the coffee, he hadn't even tasted it.

In his office, Captain Warner Conway was standing in front of his own desk, looking at his chair. A sigh went through his body. "Warner Conway," he said softly to the chair behind his desk, "you are indeed a horse's ass!" And he sighed again and felt the smile coming onto his face. It was a game he occasionally played to keep himself from becoming stuffy. For the most part, Flora Conway kept him from losing himself in his job, but now and again Conway found he needed this moment for a laugh at himself, and his role in guiding the destiny of other men. Indeed, as his wife had told him more than once, a serious attitude was fine, but it was more useful when mixed with appropriate humor. Certainly, Conway had known that all along, but, as was often the case, it took Flora to remind him.

The damp morning began to fall from his shoulders

as he reached for his box of cigars. Seated behind his desk now, he had just struck a match when the knock came at the door.

"Come," he called out, and Ben Cohen entered, carrying a telegraph flimsy and accompanied by Windy Mandalian. Seeing the look on Cohen's face, Conway knew the news was bad.

"Captain, the Sioux hit another wood detail. Boyle and Pickens are dead. The men are coming in now. Windy rode on ahead." For the moment, Cohen wasn't even aware of the dispatch from Regiment he was holding in his hand.

"When?"

Windy answered the question. "Dawn. Up by that long draw that feeds into Antelope Creek."

"Not the same place as before," Conway said, looking at the big wall map. "When they got Flanagan. How many were they?"

"A dozen," Windy replied as he pushed his hat back on his head. "They're Sioux, and some of the men recognized them. I was out with Tall Runner and heard the firing. They took off when I come in with my Sharps." He paused. "I seen Young Bear and Cricket."

"Those two again! What the hell is Cut Hand up to!" Conway turned a puzzled look on his scout and first sergeant. "We're right in the middle of delicate negotiations on the treaty, for God's sake!"

"Maybe them two have busted away from Cut Hand," Windy said. "Or on the other hand," he went on, shifting his chew, "the old boy might be fixin' to slicker us."

Conway sighed and nodded grimly.

"Captain, I've gone ahead and ordered a burial detail. The men will be here shortly," Cohen said.

"Right. And Ben, we'll send out First Platoon. With Windy." He looked at the scout. "You'll go to Little Cat Creek and see just what the hell is going on. But it will be full diplomacy; we don't want to damage the treaty at this point. It could be that Cut Hand's on the up-and-up."

"What about Kincaid, Captain? He ain't here so who you got to officer that platoon?" Windy asked.

"Ben, I want to see Lieutenant Fitzgerald. Right away."

"Yes, sir." And Ben Cohen, still holding the message from Regiment in his hand, saluted and left the room.

"Dammit!" said Conway. "Damn Regiment and their goddamn housekeeping!"

Second Lieutenant Fitzgerald, on his first tour of duty, was not long out of West Point. Still green in the ways of the frontier, he was considered by both Conway and Kincaid a good man, in need of seasoning, but not lacking in courage or humility, and he was bright. The men liked him. He stayed pretty close to the book—sometimes too close, Conway and Kincaid thought—but they knew that was his youth.

"You'll take Olsen and First Platoon," Conway was saying as he faced his junior officer within an hour after the news of the wood-detail attack had come in. "I don't expect Lieutenant Kincaid back from Stambaugh for a while, and Olsen knows the men like a farmer knows his own potato patch."

"Yes, sir. I know Olsen knows the Sioux, too."

"And you'll have Windy."

Fitzgerald nodded, relieved at having good support. It was no easy thing, stepping into Matt Kincaid's shoes.

"Sir, I understand that some of the Indians have been identified by the men."

Conway nodded. "You're not in an easy spot, Fitz. I mean, it would be a simple matter if all you had on your hands was a shooting match. But I must remind you that we're still working at the treaty with the Sioux, and we don't want to upset it by starting a big fracas. So keep talking."

"I understand, sir."

"I hope you do. Know that in dealing with an enemy—especially out here—the most difficult part is keeping your patience."

"I appreciate that, Captain," Fitzgerald said, his unlined face shining with sincerity.

"At the same time, be ready for any fighting you might have to take on." Conway studied his young officer for a moment. "Be prepared for anything, even for winning your point. Only be careful that if and when you gain it, you don't push too far and lose the whole game. Remember, Cut Hand, like Sitting Bull, is one smart fellow. Do you understand what I'm telling you?"

Fitzgerald hesitated, a slight flush of color touching his smooth cheeks. "I think so, sir. Except...I'm not exactly sure what my point is, Captain."

"Yes . . . yes." Conway moved forward in his chair, rubbing his chin with his thumb knuckle. "You want satisfaction. The thing is, you won't know what to demand, or how much, until you talk with Cut Hand. You'll be thinking and dealing on your feet. I'm really cautioning you again to take your time. Don't do anything in a hurry."

"I will remember that, sir. But am I going to arrest Young Bear and Cricket? I mean, they are responsible for two dead soldiers."

Conway looked up at the ceiling as though collecting his thoughts, and then he dropped his eyes fully onto Tom Fitzgerald. "Yes, that is exactly the point. Only our friend Cut Hand might not see it quite like that. He might be figuring war is war. He might not see that killing enemies is a crime. Then, too, he might not be the one who is responsible; maybe Young Bear and Cricket were on their own." He paused, and a wry smile was on his face. "I could go on."

Fitzgerald grinned suddenly—like a boy, Conway thought. "I think I understand, sir."

Conway stood up and offered his hand. "Good luck, Fitz."

"Thank you, sir."

"Just remember what I said about not going too fast. You can be sure Cut Hand will be taking his time."

"I understand, sir," Fitzgerald said again.

Conway remained looking at the closed door. He was thinking of the young officer's last words. "I hope you do," he said. "I hope you do understand."

His eyes were still on the door when there came another knock, and when he called out, Cohen walked in.

"Sir, a dispatch from Regiment. It came in just before Windy Mandalian, so I held it."

"More whiskey talk?" Conway sat down at his desk as Ben Cohen placed the message before him.

"No, sir. A civilian law officer from California has contacted Regiment about someone he believes might have enlisted under an assumed name. It appears to be a routine check—so far," Ben Cohen added. "At least Regiment is treating it that way."

Conway's eyebrows lifted. "You're thinking it might affect us?" He had still not looked down at the dispatch, but held his eyes on Ben Cohen's face.

"I'm not sure, Captain."

"Do they have any lead on his name?"

"The name of the man being looked for is Gatty, but it could be anything now. They don't mention any specific lead."

"Are you thinking what I'm thinking?"

"Yes, sir, I am."

"Why do they want him? What's the charge?" Conway dropped his eyes to the message in front of him. Slowly he picked up the dispatch and began reading it.

Ben Cohen was standing very still as he said, speaking to the captain's bent head, "The charge is manslaughter sir."

• • •

"You're going to be all right. You'll be fine." Private Tom Tooth got to his feet and stood looking down at Coy Flanagan, lying in his bunk in the guest barracks.

"Wish I could get rid of this fucking head," Flanagan said, his brow furrowed in pain.

"You damn near did," Tooth replied, and the boy had to grin.

"Don't make me laugh, Tooth. It hurts too damn much."

"Get some sleep," Tooth said, and turned and walked to the door of the room that opened into a small corridor leading to the parade. He was stopped by Flanagan's voice, and turned to face the young man.

Flanagan's eyes were still small with the pain he was holding. "Am I really going to be all right?"

"You're going to be fine," Tooth said.

"Tooth..."

"Yeah?"

"Thanks, Tooth."

"No charge," Tooth said, and he walked down the corridor and out onto the parade.

It was still early in the day. The rain had stopped, and he smelled again the odors of the new day penetrating the high, dry mountain air. Yes, it was good here. The altitude agreed with him. It had been the right thing to come here.

Still, he was not so sure he'd done right by Flanagan. He had risked it. He had acted on impulse. He had always acted on impulse and, damn it, it had always gotten him into trouble. He'd be put into the company report for sure, or whatever records went to Regiment. He wasn't at all certain about army organization, but he had an idea that all the officers knew everything about all the enlisted men. Something like that. Certainly what he had done with Flanagan would attract attention, which was exactly what he didn't want. Hell, he had joined the army to hide, and now he would surely be found. Tooth felt the palms of his hands sweating now as his thoughts churned. What a fool he'd been!

He had just crossed the parade and was approaching the stables when Malone and Dobbs came running toward him. At the same moment, Reb McBride's bugle cut into the cool, wet, gray air.

"Get your ass moving, Tooth," Malone called out. "We're riding out—First Platoon with Mr. Fitzgerald."

Suddenly, Tooth felt his heart lift. And then he was running toward the barracks for his rifle and his field gear, while his mind raced. Thank God for action; then he wouldn't have the thoughts. Maybe if things got active enough, he wouldn't have to keep thinking about Melissa. Tooth felt his eyes sting again, and he wiped the thought of Melissa forcibly from his mind. Then, just as he picked up his Springfield and prepared to run out to the stable for his horse, she was there again. She was there, sharp as a cameo, lying on the bed, her face twisted in agony, while the life pumped out of her with each dying breath and spurt of blood. And there was nothing he could do for her. Nothing. There wasn't a damned thing he could do. How many times he had gone over it, over and over and over...

A sob burst from him as he ran to the door of the barracks and out onto the parade.

Fifteen minutes later, First Platoon was riding through the gate, and Private Tom Tooth once again had control of himself. No one would have guessed what he had been going through for those past few minutes, nor what he had been going through for the past months. He looked serene, as he always did, riding now behind Malone and next to Stretch Dobbs in the column of twos. But he was thinking that with luck there would be a battle, and with luck maybe he would catch the right bullet.

Captain Conway stood with Ben Cohen, watching the last of the platoon go through the gate.

When the gate had closed, Cohen said, "What shall I send Regiment, Captain? Or shall I use my own initiative?"

"Your initiative has generally been good enough for me, Sergeant Cohen. Still, in this case, we'll get together and do some thinking."

"Yes, sir."

As Conway walked into his office, he wished for the second time that day that Matt Kincaid were back at Number Nine.

Realizing it was still early morning, he bit his lower lip and stood by his desk for a moment, looking at his straight-backed leather chair.

ten ————————————

"Jesus!" Gasping and clutching at the bar for support, Sweetwater John Johnson lowered his glass. His eyes filled with water, his lips quivered. "One guzzle of that there will sure fire the hair in yer nose."

He paused, then lifted his glass again. "Reckon I just wasn't ready," he said, and took a second swallow, this time without any noticeable effects.

Matt carefully took a drink. It was strong, but he had been warned by his companion, for which he was grateful.

He turned his back to the bar now, and leaning on it, supported by his elbows, he surveyed the room. It was the main room of Harold the Wizard's Good Times

Parlor, and Matt was impressed. The place was large, crowded with men and women dancing, drinking, gambling. Clearly, the Wizard was a man who leaned in the direction of size and quantity. His enormous girth bore witness to this. He was shaped like a great pear, with a pointed head and almost no shoulders at all, his weight concentrated below his chest. His feet were small, while at the other end, his bald head glistened beneath the coal-oil lamps above the bar. He had hands that were long, pointed, and soft. These were famous for fast dealing, but even more for their uncanny ability at switching flats and tops right in the midst of a dice game without the swiftest eye catching on. At the dice table, Harold the Wizard's draw was known to be the fastest in the West.

The bar itself ran the whole length of one side of the room. It consisted of rough planks set on wooden crates and upended barrels. Behind it, a huge mirror made the room appear even larger.

Listening to the fiddled strains of "Old Dan Tucker," "Chicken in the Breadtray," and other lively tunes, accompanied by the scraping of heavy boots on the wooden floor and the chanting of the caller, Matt found himself relaxing and enjoying himself.

Beside him, Sweetwater John was studying the room through the big mirror. They had decided it that way, each facing a different direction, so that they would catch the action from as many angles as possible.

"Lively," Matt said, without turning toward his companion. But he felt Sweetwater nod.

The scout said, "It's a place for people who don't

want to be where other people want 'em to be."

"If you have to have such a place," said Matt, "then I guess you couldn't beat this."

He was looking at the two wheels of fortune, the dice game, the poker tables filled with players. The room was thick with smoke, noise, the body smell of men, and now and again a faint trace of feminine perfume, an occasional brassy trill of feminine laughter.

Kincaid now found his eyes on the faro dealer setting up his bank just a few feet away from where he and Sweetwater were standing. The dealer was a thin man standing as straight as a string beneath his derby hat. He wore a brocaded vest over a striped shirt, the sleeves of which were gripped just above the elbows by two yellow garters. A big gold watch chain swung across his flat stomach and hung down as he bent over the table.

Matt enjoyed faro, though he was no gambler, playing only now and again for his own pleasure. What he liked particularly about gambling, however, and especially about faro, was watching the professionals at work. He had always admired professionalism in any field, and he found the card and dice pros especially interesting because they dealt not only with the tools of their craft, but with people.

The faro dealer was preparing his setup with his assistant, who Matt knew would be the one to pay and collect the bets, and his casekeeper, who would manipulate the small box that contained a miniature layout with four beads running along a steel rod opposite each card. It was the casekeeper's job to move the beads along, as on a billiard counter, as the cards were played, so that the players could immediately tell what cards remained to be dealt.

Kincaid watched the exquisite care with which the faro dealer placed his layout—the suit of thirteen cards, all spades, painted on a large square of oilcloth. The cards on the layout were arranged in two parallel rows, with the ace on the dealer's left and the odd card, the seven, on his extreme right. Ample space was allowed between the rows for the players to place their bets. In the row nearest the players were the king, queen, and jack, called the "big figure," and the ten, nine, and eight. In the row nearest the dealer were the ace, deuce, and trey, the "little figure," and the four, five, and six. The six, seven and eight, Matt remembered, were called the "pot." The king, queen, ace, and deuce were called the "grand square"; the jack, three, four, and ten were the "jack square"; while the nine, eight, six, and five were the "nine square."

Now he watched the faro dealer shuffle and cut the cards and then place them face upward in the dealing box, the top of which was, of course, open. The game was ready.

"Faro!" the dealer called out. "Faro bank is open!"

And suddenly Matt felt a great urge to play. But just when he was struggling with himself, he heard the voice behind him.

"You gentlemen enjoying it?"

Turning, he found that the speaker was none other

than Harold the Wizard himself, standing on the other side of the bar.

Sweetwater grabbed the bottle of whiskey by its neck, saying, "How be you, Wizard?"

The Wizard's pasty face parted in a smile that had no humor in it. "I be fine. What can I do for you and the lieutenant, Johnson?"

Sweetwater grinned at that. "The question is what are you doing for that there back room you hustled into the minute you seen us two come in, huh?"

Harold the Wizard sniffed; his hand dropped to the bar, and he swept off a dead cigar butt that somebody had left there.

Sweetwater stuck the tip of his tongue between his lips, squinting at the Wizard. Then he said, "We are lookin' for three old buzzards who was haulin' whiskey into Muddy Gap." He nodded in Matt's direction. "Don't let that uniform lollygag you; he is off duty and is only wantin' to talk to them. He ain't one of the soldiers from where them three escaped from. You got my word on it."

"What's he doing here?" Harold the Wizard's eyes were as flat and expressionless as two nailheads.

"He is here from another fort, tryin' to fix what that damn fool colonel has gone and fucked up," Sweetwater said.

"Sounds like bullshit," the Wizard said, "and smells likewise."

"I told you, you can take my word for it," Sweetwater said. "Goddammit, you know me from old times,

109

Wizard. You mind the time I saved your ass from Big Ears Mary wanting to cut your balls off, by God!"

Matt thought he saw a tint of color mix into the pasty face of Harold the Wizard. The big man on the sober side of the bar scratched the top of his big belly and then sighed. A button popped off his shirt and made a clicking sound as it struck the glass holding Sweetwater John's whiskey.

"Enjoy the premises," the Wizard said. "And"— nodding toward the stairs that ran up to the balcony— "sample the merchandise. It's prime, and the price is always right." He moved his huge body down the bar to attend to a customer.

"Well?" said Matt, his eyes following the huge man's retreating back. "What now?"

"We wait. Jake knows we're here. They spotted us the minute we come in, for Christ's sake."

"Jake?" Kincaid's eyebrows rose quizzically. "Who is Jake?"

"Poker Jake runs the whiskey trains, 'least in this part of the country. I figured the boys'd head for wherever Jake was, on account of the whole of the brains they got between 'em wouldn't fill a prairie dog's left hind leg."

"They are three pretty old fellows," Matt said. "I talked to them a bit back at Stambaugh."

Sweetwater's forehead shot up. *"You* talked to *them!* I can't figure it bein' anything but the other way around. Those old farts never do stop yappin'."

"They must have some use," Matt said. "Otherwise why would he hire them?"

"Who?"

"Jake," said Kincaid. "Whoever he is."

"Jake is a she," said Sweetwater John. "She ain't a he."

"A woman?"

The scout nodded.

Suddenly, Kincaid felt the man beside him start to shake. Turning his head, he realized that Sweetwater was chuckling. "That is, I reckon she's a woman. I mean, she has more'n likely not got a whanger and balls. On the other hand, Poker Jake is by God nothin' *but* balls!"

Sweetwater John burst into uncontrollable laughter at his own joke. He roared. He sagged against the planking of the bar, his knees buckling, almost folding his long body right down to the floor. He shook all over, the tears springing from his eyes. Finally, weak, gasping for air, gripping the bar for support and indeed almost upsetting it with his great weight, he subsided into a coughing attack that caused heads all over the room to turn. At length he was able to reach weakly for his drink.

"We'll have us a few drinks," the scout managed at last to say, when his laughter and coughing attack had subsided. "And we'll wait while Jake sizes us up some. She is a cautious old devil."

Kincaid had found the scout's laughter irresistible, and was now wiping his eyes. Sweetwater was like a huge child, always laughing at his own jokes and stories, delighting in his own self.

"I hope we don't have to wait too long," Matt said.

111

"Or one or both of us will be drunk as a skunk."

"Looks like somebody heard you, my friend. I see that big sonofabitch Harold signaling us to come on." And Sweetwater picked up his glass and started down toward the door at the other end of the bar, where Harold the Wizard was standing.

Matt turned to follow him, and as he did so, he saw out of the corner of his eye someone streaking up the stairway to the balcony above. He couldn't see the face, but only the man's legs, which left him with the impression of the color blue.

eleven ═══════════════

   The ride back to Stambaugh was made mostly
in silence, Kincaid and Sweetwater John Johnson each
harboring his own reflections on the meeting with Poker
Jake at Smith's Town. The day was warm; the country
had that fresh, awakening smell of a new spring, re-
minding Matt of his New England childhood. New
England and West Point, and then Texas, and now
Outpost Nine. He considered himself fortunate, not
only because of Conway and Easy Company, but because his life was so full. Yes, army duty could be,
and very often was, truly boring, not to mention grim.
But he considered those events and times to be the
trough of the wave, necessary for the appearance of

those crests that were so memorable. And there was much that was memorable.

And yet his present assignment had not been what he would call memorable, until his encounter with Hester Blue. She had been much in his mind during the visit to Smith's Town. Indeed, he had found her a marvelous sexual partner, not only supremely passionate, but sincerely touching in her simple affection. She was—yes—sweet. And he had a very strong wish for more of her.

At the same time he couldn't help wondering about her daughter. Could she be any more passionate than Hester? He doubted that anyone could be. Hester had been fire itself that night in bed. Yet Cynthia was so fantastically beautiful. Of course, he had met beautiful women who were pretty damned cold; so looks, as the saying went, didn't go all that deep. He had definitely decided to make no move in Cynthia's direction, principally because of Forsyth. The man could be a real troublemaker, of that he was sure. As for Hester Blue, she herself had settled the situation. It gave him pause as he reflected on the colonel's relationship with his wife. What could it be? Matt had a strong feeling that there was a lot more there—or less—than met the eye.

And so, he reflected, something had come through what at first appeared to be a dull, boring, political assignment, the kind he especially hated. Hester Blue had saved it from disaster. And he found himself really eager for a return engagement with the colonel's wife, at the same time not wanting it for the simple reason that should Blue find out what was happening right under his blue nose, he might well start hollering for Kincaid's scalp.

The encounter with Poker Jake had carried things into another realm. While not including sexual activity—thank God, Matt reflected with rueful humor—meeting Poker Jake had been an extraordinary event. Jake had greeted her two visitors head on, and had literally dealt her cards with guile, wry humor, sulfurous profanity, and with absolutely no expression on her wrinkled old face. Thinking about it later, Kincaid had broken out laughing. He had never met anyone like Jake, and he knew it wasn't likely he would again.

"Try your luck at three-card monte, gents?" The crackling voice had greeted them as Matt and Sweetwater walked into the Wizard's back room; one wrinkled hand reached for her glass of whiskey, the other removed the cigar from her mouth.

Sweetwater John grinned. "Jake, you an' me both know I would have about as much chancet playin' three-card monte with yerself as a fart'd have in a fire fight with the Sioux."

"I'll try a hand or two," Matt said, stepping over to the vacant chair in front of Poker Jake.

"Pick the ace," Jake said without looking up, as her eyes followed her own hands switching the cards with lightning speed. "Now you sees it, now you doesn't." Flashing the ace again, she turned it over so that only the backs of the three cards showed, all the time switching the cards. "Follow the ace. Where is the little fucker?"

Kincaid hesitated. Her hands were moving faster than those of any dealer he had ever seen.

All at once Jake slowed down. The hands moved slowly. "Here is the ace," she said, showed its face, then flipped it over. He followed her moves as she exchanged the cards slowly, their faces down. Then she sped up. Suddenly she stopped.

"For Chrissake, pick it. We ain't got all night!"

"That one in the middle."

"That one?" Jake's filthy fingernail tapped the card.

"That one."

"You are saying that is the ace."

"That's right."

"The ace of spades?"

"The ace of spades."

The cold gray eyes lifted. The wrinkled hand took the cigar from where it had been burning into the edge of the table, and raised it to the corner of the slanted mouth.

"Buster, look inside yer left pocket there."

Matt did as he was told, and pulled a card out of his pocket.

"What is it?"

He turned the card face up.

"It's the ace."

"Yer damn right it's the ace!"

"That's pretty smart," he said with a grin.

"So it ain't that there middle card."

Matt looked steadily at the old lady in front of him. "It could be."

"You mean there is two aces?"

"There could be."

"Two aces of spades?"

"I think there is."

"Put yer money on that, buster."

Matt reached into his pocket and came up with a silver dollar.

"What the fuck is that! I said I want yer *money* on it. You're accusin' me of cheatin'! Put yer *money* on that, soldier!"

"Jake—" Sweetwater John started to remonstrate.

"Shut up, you!"

"I'll add two more cartwheels and that's it." Matt's voice was hard as he carefully laid down the money, three silver dollars in a row.

"I'm covering your small change there."

He knew by then that she had of course switched it, as her fingers flipped the card toward him faceup. It was a nine.

"Three cartwheels! What kind of money is that? Wouldn't buy a bottle of cold piss in December, fer Chrissake! No wonder Custer got his ass whipped!"

Poker Jake, muttering to herself now, picked up the cards and placed them carefully on top of the deck at her elbow.

"Just wanted you two gents to know what sort of person you might be dealing with. What d'you want?"

"And I would like for you to know who it is you might be dealing with," Kincaid said, his voice clear, level, and cold, drawing an admiring glance from Sweetwater John. "I am Lieutenant Matthew Kincaid, United States Army Mounted Infantry, stationed at

Outpost Number Nine, Wyoming Territory."

"Pleased to meet you," Poker Jake muttered, her eyes meeting his from under hooded lids.

"I am not attached to Fort Stambaugh or Colonel Jonathan Blue in any way. I'm up here looking for some renegade Sioux who've been causing trouble down by Packhorse Butte."

"So? I don't have no renegade Indians in here, Lieutenant."

"The Indians were fired up with whiskey. I followed three men who were driving a whiskey train and got themselves arrested by Colonel Blue, and then escaped. You follow me?"

"I do follow you. But I am gettin' tired of listenin' to all this bullshit. Get to the point!"

Matt couldn't help it. He suddenly burst out in laughter. Sweetwater was puzzled for a moment, but then joined in. Their hostess remained as unperturbed as ever.

"Look, Jake, I want to stop the selling of whiskey to the tribes. It causes too damn much trouble. Too many people killed. I am not trying to stop whiskey being sold to the whites in the territory. But I do have orders to stop whiskey being sold to the tribes. That is what I'm trying to make clear."

"I figured that out a half hour ago, fer Chrissakes!"

"Then I need your help. That's why I'm here."

"What do you mean, you need my help!"

"I'm talking about the Indians."

"I don't sell whiskey to the Indians. You think I'm crazy? I know how they get when they drink. Nobody in his right mind would sell them whiskey."

"But they get it. And they're getting more now."

"Look, if they want to get it, they're goin' to get it."

"Somebody is selling it to them."

"You sure?"

"I am sure."

Jake's eyelids closed down over the gray eyes like alligator skin. Then they suddenly sprang open to look at Sweetwater John. "Got a notion, Sweetwater?"

"I am studyin' on it."

"Big fuckin' help that is."

"I ain't seen Otis Birdwhistle about in this good while, and I heerd too that he ain't been presentin' himself overly much," Sweetwater said.

"And you won't. I caught the sonofabitch with his hand in the till." She stopped suddenly and then continued, "When I caught him redhanded swiping money, the little bugger said he'd wished his hand was in my pants. Now what the hell do you make of that!"

"Jesus," murmured Sweetwater John.

Matt said nothing, but found a spot on the far wall to look at for a moment.

"Heard Otis was over to Rock Crossing, close by the Sioux reserve," Sweetwater said.

"You saw him?"

"I say I *heerd* he was there. Man said he was driving a Red River cart."

"Anything in it?"

"Man didn't say."

"Rock Crossing's by the UP tracks."

119

"That is so."

"Sonofabitch!"

"Be a pity," Sweetwater said, speaking softly, "if Otis Birdwhistle was to cut in on business you might have—I says *might*—with the sutler over to Rock Crossing."

"I am way ahead of you, Sweetwater," Poker Jake said, and turned to Matt. "Make a deal with you. I'll handle Birdwhistle so's the Injuns stays dry. You stop that crazy sonofabitch at Stambaugh. I don't want him bustin' up my wagons and getting the prairie drunk on good, honest liquor."

But Kincaid was already shaking his head. "Jake, I am in no position to make any deal. I'm an officer in the United States Army. No deals."

"Pretty dumb," Jake said, as cold as viper. "Exceptin', Lieutenant, you look about as dumb and as much against making any deal that will get you where you wanta go as Ulysses S. Grant musta looked when he won the War."

And to the utter astonishment of both Matt Kincaid and Sweetwater John Johnson, the corners of Poker Jake's mouth began to twitch. But, heroically, the lady declined the weakness, and her impassivity swept in again. The meeting was over.

Now, riding beside Sweetwater John as they continued on their way back to Fort Stambaugh, Matt was trying to see how he could possibly restrain Jonathan Blue from the mad crusade on which he was so devoutly engaged. He knew Poker Jake would keep her end of the bargain, provided he followed through with his, which, though not stated in words, was understood by all parties concerned.

It was midafternoon when they rode across a narrow creek and came out into a lush stand of cheatgrass.

"You been thinkin' hard enough, Lieutenant, to boil a egg," Sweetwater said as Matt drew rein.

Matt swung out of his saddle with a sigh. "Sweetwater, the saying is that there are a whole lot of ways to skin a cat. I'd like to know just one."

Sweetwater stepped down from the dappled gray and ground-hitched it. "Good to stretch," he said. "I bin studyin' it, too," he went on. "Been wonderin' who that soldier feller could of been, back at the Wizard's."

"The one going upstairs? When we were on our way in to meet Jake?"

"You spotted him?"

"Not really. Just caught him out of the corner of my eye. Why?"

"Couldn't see if he was one I knew from Stambaugh, but I was wonderin'. On account of Harold the Wizard's Place don't usually cater to soldiers, since most couldn't afford to buy one of them gals a pair of drawers, leave alone gettin' her on her back."

"What do the enlisted men do for it, then?"

"They go to Maggie's, in the back room of the Star Saloon. Maggie's is Maggie—and that's it. She is the most rundown, beat-up, fucked-out whore I have ever laid eyes on in my whole entire life. 'Course, there *is* the Indians," Sweetwater added, "and a lot of the boys lock horns with them. Better, cleaner than that Maggie, I'd say for a fact."

"It could've been one of Blue's officers," Matt said.

Sweetwater John spat suddenly at a prairie dog that had appeared a short distance away. But his aim fell far short.

"Be a funny, wouldn't it," he said, "if it was old Jonathan Bluenose hisself, gettin' his freight shifted, huh?" And he cocked an eye at Matt, who had taken out a cigar and was lighting it.

"The colonel doesn't seem to me to be the sort who would patronize such a place as Harold's," he said. "Though it would be funny, as you say."

Sweetwater snorted. "Shit, Lieutenant, with a wife like his, it's a wonder he ain't visitin' Maggie's."

twelve ⸻⸻⸻

By late afternoon the column of men and horses had left the prairie, and now they rode up through thick stands of pine, spruce, hemlock, and fir. The trees were stunted as they approached the rimrocks, the result of storms and heavy winter drifts. The horses picked their way slowly along the hard trail, their shod hooves ringing in the silent day. Windy Mandalian was leading them over a shortcut to Little Cat Creek.

At nightfall they bivouacked right under the giant rimrocks overlooking the broad sweep of land down to the river. It was cold, and the men huddled together with their coffee.

Malone rose and refilled his mug.

"Wonder how Flanagan is doin'," he said, looking over at Pony Tom Tooth as he settled himself again.

Tooth was smoking his pipe, seated beside Stretch Dobbs on the other side of the circle.

Taking the pipe out of his mouth, he said, "You can pray for him, Malone."

The Irishman's jaw dropped. "Pray for him? You mean he might not make it?"

"No, no. I meant you can pray for him. Pray for us all, is how I meant it." Tooth lifted his somber eyes to the sky. "Flanagan is going to be just fine. But he isn't going to live forever. Nor will any of us."

"Jesus God, you're a cheerful bastard!" Malone spat in disgust.

"Sorry, Malone. Just feeling my old bones in this cold air."

"That's all right, Pony boy," Malone said with largesse. "It's that damn McClellan that does it to a man. I'll bet it ain't like them Pony Express saddles, huh? Real small, I've heard they used to be. But soft."

Tooth found himself grinning in spite of his gloomy thoughts. "It was rough riding, even on those special light saddles," he said.

"How long did it take you, Tooth?" Reb McBride asked.

"We picked up a New York wire in St. Joe and had it at the Alta telegraph office in San Francisco within ten days."

"Sounds a helluva ways."

"Two thousand miles. We'd average two hundred a day in summer, less in winter."

"And your ride...is how long?" Holzer asked, slamming out his words along with a generous portion of saliva.

"Each rider did about a hundred and twenty five miles, sometimes more."

"Jesus..."

Tooth's words had brought a touch of awe to the group. The name "Pony Express" was wrapped in romance for these men. Although it had existed for only a year and a half during their childhoods, at the same time that the Civil War was beginning, it had spawned far more than its share of legends and heroes.

Tooth felt good talking about his adventures. He had loved the job. Just a kid at the time himself, he had grown into a man in a month or two. At that, he had not been as young as another rider, Bill Cody, who was only fourteen.

"How long did it take you to change horses at them stations?" Stretch Dobbs asked.

"Two minutes," Tooth said. "Even less, if possible. You jumped off, grabbed your *mochila*— what you carried the mail in—and you were on your next horse and away before the first one had come to a halt." He chuckled at their awe. "Oh, the horse handler had a cup of coffee and a sandwich ready—and some cookies we'd eat on the way." He paused. "Used to come right through the South Pass," he went on. "Never thought I'd ever come back to this country, once I'd left. You never know. You just never know."

Tooth continued to sit where he was, smoking his pipe, drinking coffee, looking up at the stars. Yes, it was good, talking about the Express. He seldom talked about it. But it had been a bright time, a brilliant time for him. The diamond of his life. No, he didn't mean that. The setting maybe, but not the diamond. The diamond had been Melissa.

Oh, God, he was thinking. *Oh, God, I don't know if I can stand any more.* He knew how difficult it would be to sleep. It was the main reason he worked so hard—to be tired enough to escape at night. Except there wasn't really any escape, for there were always dreams. Or there were long hours lying awake, thinking of her, feeling her, longing for her.

And now, again, his eyes on those distant stars, those other worlds, over it. Would it ever go away? Would it ever get settled? Maybe when he was dead? He continued to sit there long after the men had rolled into their bedding, thinking of Melissa and the baby, reliving every detail of what he had done to save her life after Doc Webster had told him she couldn't bear a child and live. And how he had watched her die, and had died with her. Except that he hadn't.

Second Lieutenant Fitzgerald accepted a mug of coffee from Sergeant Gus Olsen and looked toward the eastern horizon. The first light was moving behind the mountains. He had watched the mountains the evening before, as night approached—the copper hue along the great mountain peaks, the blood-red clouds, and the fading of the light, not only along the horizon but where he'd been standing. So soft it had been, so very silent. Truly, he'd thought, it was a unique silence, and for a moment he felt something pull at his heart, and to his astonishment he wondered if he was going to cry. But Fitzgerald had remembered that he was a soldier—and not only a soldier, but an officer, and proud of the fact. The dying of the day had instantly become just another sunset. Now, as the dawn penetrated the great sky, he felt just an instant of what he had experienced the evening before, something like a breath brushing him, and he was again moved. But he suddenly thought of the two dead men, and Flanagan scalped and covered in blood, and he gulped down the rest of the hot coffee and faced the men who were breaking camp.

"I want every man on full alert, and I want everyone to remember that we are still under treaty negotiations with the Sioux. That means that despite what happened, we will not provoke any attack. No one is to fire a weapon unless I give the order!"

Fitzgerald had walked several paces along the line of men as he spoke. Now he turned back to Olsen. "Sergeant, give the order to mount up. No talking, no smoking. It will be column of twos."

Windy Mandalian, kneeing his little blue roan in close to Fitzgerald, said, "Suppose the two of us go in alone, Lieutenant. Leave the platoon with Olsen a ways off."

Fitzgerald threw a puzzled glance at the scout. "You know the Sioux a lot better than I do, Windy, but why? They could grab the two of us and hold us prisoners."

"They could, but they won't. We will be dealing with an Indian who is smart enough to get us coming to him on a peace mission. Cut Hand isn't going to start any fighting, and if we bring the platoon in too close, it's just gonna make some of them warriors nervous-like."

"I don't understand, then, why Cut Hand, if he's so powerful and smart, like everybody tells me, doesn't just tell his warriors to behave themselves. I mean, hell, this is the third time Young Bear and Cricket have broken out—first at Hanrahan's, then when they scalped Flanagan, and now killing Boyle and Pickens."

"Been tryin' to explain to you, Lieutenant, the way it works," Windy said patiently, shifting his chew in his mouth and shifting his body in his stock saddle at the same time. "The real chiefs—like Cut Hand—don't tell anyone what to do. They lead by persuasion, and damn seldom give a direct order to anybody, unless there's an emergency. It ain't like our army."

"Yes, you've told me that before."

"See, you know it's like the way they break their horses. They don't sack 'em and halter-break 'em and treat 'em rough the way white bronc-stompers do; they don't try to break the animal's spirit. They lead their people the same way. So I am suggesting we try to understand that that's the way their minds work, and we might help ourselves keep our hair on by going along with it."

"I appreciate what you say, Windy. You know I have always respected your judgment, but do you really think what you're suggesting is the best way? I want to be sure, for both of us, and for all of us. Do you really think that's the way?"

Windy moved his roan closer, squinting now at the young lieutenant as he canted his head. The rate of his chewing did not vary.

"I don't get paid to think, Lieutenant," he said. "I get paid to *know*."

He had promised that when the grass was as high as the width of his hand, he would make the offering. Now it was the Moon When the Ponies Shed, and the grass was indeed a hand's width high. And so he had made the offering of sweet grass.

It was good. Ah, it was good to be in the old way, taking time, doing everything slowly and well. Now, surrounded by the great ocean of the *Wasichus,* it was difficult to allow time for things, time for what was necessary: to grow, to become, to die. The *Wasichus* were always hurrying, always rushing here and there, forcing, demanding, so that everything became fixed, hard, with no breath, no life in it anymore. And who would be left, he wondered. Who would be left to remember the true way, when all had become the lying, and when what was Above had become lost and forgotten to the People? Who would remind them? How would they remember that there was another way?

He had been standing with his arms outstretched toward the rising sun, singing the special prayer to the Great Spirit. Now, lowering his arms, he remained still, in the special silence that always brought the holy day. He stood motionless, and yet in movement—alive to all that was in him and around him—still praying in his mind to all that breathed. And as he listened to the life, actually seeing the air in which he was standing, and now opening to the precious movement of sweet life coursing through him and everything around him, the tears flowed from his eyes and down his bronze cheeks and into the hanging braids of his crow-black hair.

Cut Hand was still standing there by the little creek near his lodge, in the first light of the sun, when the crier ran through the camp, calling out that the Pony soldiers were coming.

thirteen ═══════════

Dinner in the colonel's parlor had been thoroughly enjoyable. This time Ned Forsyth had not been present. Matt wondered if the adjutant was unwell.

"Captain Forsyth has taken an overnight pass," Blue told him. "He does that every now and again, just like any of us. We shall simply have to struggle along without our adjutant."

Had it been Forsyth, Matt wondered now, that he and Sweetwater had seen at Harold the Wizard's? But the question didn't go very far. Matt was much too pleased to find himself once again in the company of Cynthia Blue, especially without Forsyth.

"So good to have you back with us, Lieutenant Kincaid," the adorable girl was saying. "We thought we had lost you."

Matt felt Hester Blue's eyes on him at that moment, and he turned to look at her, but she instantly looked down to her plate.

"I wouldn't think of getting lost from either you or your parents, Miss Blue," Matt said gallantly.

He and Sweetwater John had just returned from Smith's Town that same day, and the invitation to dinner at the colonel's had been presented immediately on his arrival. Certainly it was a miraculous change, after his adventure with Poker Jake and Sweetwater John Johnson.

The evening was quiet, keeping its own pace. The food was good—unfortunately lacking wine to assist its digestion—but Matt was by no means suffering. The food he needed was sitting right across the table from him. While Hester Blue kept her eyes away from him during the whole of the evening, her daughter behaved in quite the opposite fashion. Her glances couldn't have been more attentive.

"Did you ever meet Mackenzie down there?" Jonathan Blue cut abruptly into his thoughts, and for a moment Kincaid was at a loss.

"Down in Texas," Blue snapped impatiently. "Thought you might have. Famous man!"

"Colonel Ranald Mackenzie, sir? Of course, I know who he is. Met him once. We had dealings with the Fourth Cavalry." Matt nodded agreeably as Blue's remarks brought to memory the intrepid Mackenzie.

"You mentioned Custer earlier, I believe," Blue went on. "I believe Mackenzie is tougher, with all due respect to the 'boy general.' You know, Mackenzie made brigadier general before he was twenty-five, like Custer. But they were different by a country mile. Mackenzie was a dour Scot. Never married. Unlike Custer, he didn't favor the ladies. Eh? He was an enigma. Lonely. Ascetic. But tough, I say!"

He paused, his hairy little fingers drumming alongside his plate, then went on, "I know the men in the Fourth used to put on their chevrons with hooks and eyes; he'd bust 'em right in the field for the least infraction. I say, the *least* infraction! The army needs much more of that!"

He paused, head bowed as he searched his memory. "You know, his wiping out Dull Knife's Cheyenne village on Crazy Woman Creek made him the first to avenge Custer. Yes, Ranald Mackenzie is a tougher man even than George Armstrong Custer!" The colonel's eyes were glowing with admiration as he spoke.

The evening ended early. Though he'd had a long ride back from Smith's Town, Kincaid wasn't the least bit tired, thanks to the presence of Miss Blue. He found it difficult to understand why Ned Forsyth would take a pass away from the post when he had something like the exquisite Cynthia at hand.

The evening offered one more memorable moment besides those he had enjoyed feasting his eyes upon Cynthia Blue. The colonel, following him to the door to see him off, suddenly tripped on the edge of the carpet and went flying into his wife, nearly knocking her down. Blue swiftly regained his balance. Hester righted herself with a bit of difficulty. Blue's composure was awesome.

"My dear, please do *not* stand in my way like that!"

Hester Blue seemed to fade into the background as Matt, forcing himself to conceal the laugh that almost broke from him, shook hands with Cynthia and took his departure.

Feeling restless, and not at all like sleeping, Kincaid took a while strolling around the parade, hoping that the girl might appear. But she did not. Finally he headed for his quarters, half wondering if Hester Blue would pay him another visit.

He had just started to get ready for bed when there came a knock at the door. For a moment he wondered if it could be Cynthia, but instantly wiped out the thought, telling himself she would never be that forward. Of course, it would be Hester. To his delight, it turned out to be Cynthia Blue who was standing in his doorway.

"I apologize for disturbing you at this late hour, Lieutenant Kincaid, but I so wanted to talk to you, and it wasn't really possible with Father and Mother present. If this isn't a good time, could we perhaps make it another time, maybe tomorrow?"

"The time is just right, Miss Blue. Please come in."

He stepped back to allow her to enter, and as she moved into the room, two of the walls were filled with her shadow thrown by the kerosene lamp.

Matt offered her the only chair, and placed himself on the edge of the bed.

134

"I'm very happy to get to talk with you, Miss Blue. What may I do for you?"

"First, please call me Cynthia."

"I'm Matt."

The dimple on her cheek showed as she smiled at him for just a second, and then she was serious again.

"It's about Ned—er, Captain Forsyth." She looked down at her hands lying in her lap. She had removed her cape, and her bare throat shone in the light thrown by the lamp. "I don't want to burden you, Matt, a virtual stranger, with my problems. But I need advice. And I can't go to Daddy."

It flashed through his mind that perhaps she had gotten pregnant. What else could be of such clandestine importance, he asked himself.

"If I can help you in any way, Cynthia..."

"I am so grateful to have you to talk to."

His eyes were following her lips as she spoke, and he could barely resist getting to his feet, walking over to her chair and kissing her. At the same time he was fully aware of the erection that was pressing so furiously against his trousers that he had to keep his hands in his lap to hide it.

"You say it's something to do with Ned?"

"Ned wants to marry me, and I—Well, Dad and Mother want me to marry him."

"But you don't want to."

She nodded, her head bowed.

"You don't love him?"

"I not only don't love him, he makes my flesh crawl."

135

The words came out with a sudden vehemence that startled him.

"You surprise me," Matt said frankly. "I'd thought,—well, I don't know what I thought."

"You thought we were...together, Ned and I."

"Yes. More or less. In fact..." He grinned.

"In fact, what?" Her eyes were wide as she looked at him questioningly.

"In fact, Ned took a certain amount of time to tout me off you."

At his words, the color rushed into her face and she flared. "He has some nerve!"

"In any case, Cynthia, I am absolutely certain you won't have a moment's trouble finding another young man. I'm sure you have to beat them off." And he grinned amiably at her.

"I have had to beat Ned Forsyth off, let me tell you. He is an animal! A beast!"

"How so? You mean he doesn't take no for an answer?"

Suddenly there were tears in her eyes, and she reached to her pocket for a handkerchief. Matt watched her cheeks glistening in the lamplight as the tears flowed silently from those big brown eyes.

"I mean," she said, controlling herself with an effort, "I couldn't begin to tell you what he has asked, what he's—yes, *demanded* I should do with him." And she looked fiercely across the few feet that separated them.

"What do you mean—do with him?"

Her eyes dropped again to her lap. "I'm a bit ashamed

to say. It's rather horrible. I mean, he is a vile man. Vile!"

Matt watched her quietly for a moment.

"I just don't know how to get rid of him. That's the problem."

"Tell him no."

"But I've done that. So many times."

Kincaid leaned forward. "But Cynthia," he said gently. "You have to *mean* no."

Her eyes were the biggest he had ever seen as she stared back at him. "You don't believe I've said no and meant no. Do you know what he wanted me to do?"

"I suppose he wanted first of all to get into bed with you," Matt said. He was having difficulty controlling the pounding he felt in his throat and chest, while his erection was driving savagely into his trousers. What sort of woman was she, he wondered.

"If it had been just that . . . well . . ." She hesitated only a moment and then said, "Maybe I would have with somebody, but certainly not with Ned Forsyth. I had no feeling for him like that. The thing is, he wanted me to . . . something else."

"I see." Matt regarded her slowly. He was not at all sure he *did* see. "Uh, look, I don't suppose you could be a little more explicit? I'm not trying to be nosy, butting into your personal business—but you did ask me to help you."

"Yes, I did."

There followed a long pause. Her eyes, which had been looking into his, now dropped to his hands, which were still lying in his lap, still trying casually to cover his erection.

The silence continued while she kept her eyes on the backs of his hands. When he moved his hands, her eyes did not follow them, but remained staring at the protrusion at his crotch. Without even realizing what he was doing, he had risen and stepped over to where she sat, and now stood directly in front of her.

He was looking down at the top of her head. She looked up at him and her hand reached up and touched the great bulge that was almost in her face.

"I can be more explicit," she said. "I'll show you what he wanted."

It was late when Cynthia left. Her demonstration of what Ned Forsyth had demanded of her had been all that Matt could possibly have dreamed of. And then, later, to his utter delight, she received him in the customary, orthodox manner. It was an exhilarating evening, the best of times, he decided as he climbed happily back into bed after seeing her to the door.

Just before he fell asleep, he spent a moment puzzling over the question of which of the Blues pleased him more, Cynthia or Hester. The daughter had certainly inherited Hester Blue's delightful and adroit animality regarding country matters.

Suddenly his thoughts turned to Forsyth and his demands on Cynthia. He was certain now that it had been Forsyth going upstairs at the Wizard's. Well, it made sense. If he wasn't getting it at home, he'd best look for it somewhere else.

He was suddenly wide awake, sitting straight up in bed. It had become absolutely clear to him how he was going to deal with Colonel Bluenose—or rather, how Sweetwater John Johnson was going to.

fourteen

"I have given my word to Captain Conway that I will not fight—nor will my people—so long as the talk of peace is with us both."

Cut Hand's words were measured and firm as he spoke in the seated circle with his headmen and the white soldiers.

Fitzgerald had been immediately impressed with the chief's bearing, his dignity, and the careful way he spoke.

"We honor your word, Cut Hand," he said in reply. "And we understand, as you have explained, that the two warriors—Young Bear and Cricket—were acting against your orders." Fitzgerald paused, feeling suddenly nervous under the Indian's steady gaze, which seemed to be directed right between his eyes. He half turned toward Windy, and then resumed, taking a strong grip on himself, "I am saying, however, that the two warriors must be turned over to me, to the army. I must take them to the fort, where they will be tried fairly and, if found guilty, punished."

The silence that fell in the council tipi then was something tangible. Finally, after a very long moment had passed, Cut Hand spoke.

"That I cannot do, Lieutenant."

"But you must!" Fitzgerald broke out. "They have broken the law!"

He felt Windy's restraining hand on his arm, and then was totally thrown as he was aware of the blood rushing in embarrassment to his face.

Nothing changed in the expression on the Sioux chief's face. He continued to look at Fitzgerald.

At length he said, "The law? They have broken the law, you say, Lieutenant? The white man's law? But we are at war with the white man, and to kill an enemy is not breaking a law."

"*Ho! Ho!*" said several voices in the circle.

"But we are trying to work out a treaty," Fitzgerald said.

"Yes. While doing that, the whites continue to move onto our land, the land given to us from other treaties. And they bring the whiskey. Where is your law then?"

"But the warriors killed two soldiers!" Fitzgerald insisted.

"In war, men are killed." Cut Hand looked at Windy.

"We have broken no law. The only law is the law from Above. And we have not broken that."

Windy had remained silent for the most part throughout the conversation, letting Fitzgerald make his own point, but now he began to speak.

"Cut Hand, the thing is, the army wants them two— Cricket and Young Bear—punished. I know, same as you, they was acting out of line. But they have got to be punished."

"They will be punished, Windy. That is certain. For they have again disobeyed, and they cannot be trusted. To this I agree, and so do the others." He moved his hand slightly to include his headmen, who muttered softly in agreement. "They will be punished by their people. For they have taken the whiskey and behaved in a bad way, thus hurting the People. But that is for us to do. It is not for the soldier whites."

Cut Hand paused. His eyes went to Fitzgerald and back to the scout.

"Windy, you know our ways. Tell the lieutenant. He asks of us something we cannot do. We cannot give up our people to *Wasichu* justice—for there is no such thing. We will not give away Young Bear and Cricket."

"Ho! Ho!"

"But you said you were going to punish them anyway," Fitzgerald insisted. "So what is the difference?"

"They will be punished, Lieutenant. They behaved wrongly, and for that they will be punished. But by the hand of their own people, not by the white man. Now we will rest a moment. I have spoken."

He closed his eyes, and the headmen shifted in their places, turning toward Cut Hand. Presently they began to converse in their own language.

At a signal from Windy, Fitzgerald got up and followed him outside the tent.

"What's going on now?" Fitzgerald asked, the moment they were outside.

"They're talking it over," Windy said.

"You understand their language, don't you?"

"They'll decide a way of working it out. They don't want to fight. But they sure as hell ain't gonna back down." Windy grinned. "I got a notion the old boy already had his plan long before we even walked into his tipi."

"I don't understand why it can't be simple. Why do they always make everything so complicated?"

Windy let a smile play over his face as he regarded Fitzgerald's wrinkled forehead, his tense shoulders. "But it's us who is complicated, Lieutenant. Our talk about law don't mean a damn thing to them. They're talking about a man's honor and his place in the whole outfit—the universe." He paused to spit. "See, all you and me got to do is understand them."

Fitzgerald's young face reddened. The scout had spoken kindly, but he didn't understand, and he wasn't at all sure he hadn't somehow bungled.

"Justice is very simple," he maintained. "And the Sioux and the other Indians have to be brought to see that."

Windy Mandalian's Adam's apple moved once in his long neck. "Lieutenant—you don't mind if I call you 'son,' do you? I mean, I'm damn near old enough to be your paw, and I been living in this country since long before your own maw and paw even thought of you." He paused, sniffing, reaching for his tobacco. "That stuff they smoke is hard on a chewing man," he said.

When he had cut himself a sizable chew and worked it around in his jaws so he could handle it, he went on, "Son, it's like this. Them fellers in there, they got their own way of doin' things. Let 'em work it out. What's the point here, anyways? We don't want any more raids, right?"

"Sure. But I don't see—"

"So it don't matter who's right or who's wrong. What matters is to not have any more raids. You get me?"

Fitzgerald was puzzling on that when one of the headmen came out of the tipi and signaled.

"What's happening now?"

"They've settled something," Windy said.

When they reentered the lodge and had seated themselves again, Cut Hand took up the pipe that was resting on the special buffalo chip in front of him.

"We will smoke together," he said, and he began preparing the pipe.

At Harold the Wizard's Good Times Parlor, the action was lively. There was nothing new in that. But it was new for one of the two extraordinary figures seated in a back room of the establishment.

Colonel Jonathan Blue, wearing spotless fringed

buckskin, topped by a widebrimmed Stetson hat, sat fully erect in his straight-backed wooden chair, facing the greasy, buckskinned, fabled scout of the plains, Sweetwater John Johnson.

"You say they'll be here," Blue was saying, clipping his words as though he were standing in front of a regiment.

"That's the idea, Colonel," the scout drawled. "But we got to be patient. Can't rush things."

"I am the soul of patience, dammit, Johnson! I do not need your conceited lecturing. We are here on a mission, and I wish to execute that mission with neatness and dispatch. Thus, I want it absolutely clear that I am only engaging in this social frivolity as a means toward my end."

The old scout's eyebrows rose. "Your end? You talkin' about your ass, Colonel? Or the end of your life?" And Sweetwater's eyes narrowed as he studied the Colonel's meaning.

"I am talking about my aim, my purpose, Sweetwater—I mean, Johnson. Scout Johnson, in fact. Try to understand me. It will save a lot of time." He pushed an enormous sigh all the way through his body.

"Jesus," muttered the man who, people claimed, would most assuredly find his way into the history books, along with Jim Bridger, Custer, Kit Carson, Fremont, and other such colorful individuals.

And indeed, the exploits of Sweetwater John Johnson were numerous and provocative, not to mention apocryphal. Still, there was enough meat to handle the sauce. He had fought the Kiowa, the Sioux, and a host of other hostiles including both bandits and lawmen, not to mention angry husbands. He had trapped, surveyed, guided wagon trains, shot bear and bison and elusive Rocky Mountain sheep, survived Comanche torture, and lived to tell of Fremont's disastrous expedition across the Rockies below the thirty-eighth parallel in the dreadful winter of '48–'49. Sweetwater had done everything, been everything, and, according to more than one humorist, "done *tolt* everythin'!"

Windy Mandalian, one of the more acute observers of this colorful figure had put it that in Sweetwater reposed a tongue that could "sweet-talk a minister out of his Sunday morning collection." But at the moment, the venerable scout was simply enjoying himself.

"I am telling you, Colonel, Smith's Town is for sure a town with the hair on."

Jonathan Blue, trim as a new-boiled egg in that spanking frontier costume, responded sharply to the scout's observation. "Again—and must I go on repeating myself needlessly?—I say, again I am driven to declare that I am not as interested in Smith's Town, or in this vile resort of alleged pleasure, as I am in apprehending those damned whiskey peddlers! I want to see them. I am taking you at your word that they will appear on these premises. It is why I have agreed to your madcap scheme of dressing up in this ridiculous attire! Certainly it is no place for me to appear in uniform!"

The colonel glared at the huge figure sitting across the table as he lifted his glass of sarsaparilla and drank deeply. "Ah, that's better!" His eyes dropped to the

147

sleeve of his buckskin jacket and a trace of a smile flitted over his small tight face.

"Custer used to wear buckskin, you know, Johnson." He brought up his hand to stop any protest from Sweetwater. "I know you hunted buffalo with the general, and you don't quite favor all the publicity he has received; but I am telling you that George Armstrong Custer was a man of simple demeanor, rather like myself. Never put on airs when he was out of uniform. Indeed, he often wore frontier apparel. In this, I say, he revealed his true colors as a man of the people. I, however, favor military habit the more. In this I'd place myself closer to Mackenzie than Custer."

And once more he addressed himself to his glass of sarsaparilla while Sweetwater John, softly belching alcohol in his direction, looked upon the colonel's glass with horror and loathing.

"Colonel, I know you favor that sassy-sprilla stuff. But it sure makes me queasy to even watch you. It is a hell of a brew. You know, I mind the time I was up to Fort Phil Kearny when Red Cloud had the soldiers pinned into the fort that winter, what was a real cold shitpisser, and he was scarin' the shit outta the whole fuckin' army that he was gonna wipe out the fort. Well, there was this here feller—a old muleskinner he was—an' he was drinkin' that sassy-sprilla stuff like crazy at the sutler's and by God—you got to believe it, Colonel—he up and developed the blind staggers! I swears it on a stack of Bibles! Fell down right there in the snow one night it was at least forty below. Come morning, he was froze stiff as a whanger that ain't had action in six months." He paused for effect, then went on, "We unfreezed that fella with honest-to-God whiskey. He gave thanks to the Almighty for that kindness!"

Sweetwater paused, wiping nose and mouth in one stroke with his sleeve, following through with the back of his hand. "I mean, Jesus! Lay off of that stuff, Colonel!"

"Nonsense. That is pure nonsense! Just one of your crazy stories. I don't believe a word of it. Sweetwater—Johnson, I mean—by the way, how did you get that name? Should be Sweet Whiskey Johnson, I'd say." And he suddenly broke into a shout of laughter, causing the old scout first to stare in awe, and then, catching the distinct odor of alcohol on the colonel's breath—to smile with pleasure.

"Colonel, work your way down another glass or two, and might be you an' me could visit some of the fine gals they got in this place."

Jonathan Blue's eyes widened. "Johnson, you stop that idiotic talk. I suppose you think you're funny!"

Sweetwater grinned hugely. "C'mon, Colonel, wouldn't you go for a little stuff?" The grin became a leer. "We can slip upstairs from the outside door they got for fellers like yourself what don't want to get noticed by everybody."

"You stop that! I mean right this minute. Now get me another sarsaparilla!"

Sweetwater rose to his feet, saying, "We'll have another round, Colonel." He had crossed to the door of the room as he spoke, and now he opened it and bellowed out at the bartender, "Hey, Wizard! More of the same!"

And standing in the doorway with his back to the colonel, he made a fist with his thumb straight up, and watched the smile on Harold the Wizard's face as he reached for the whiskey bottle and poured generously into first one glass, and then more carefully into the second glass, which he then completed with sarsaparilla.

"You done right good, son," Windy was saying as he and Fitzgerald walked away from the Sioux council lodge and crossed the cottonwood grove.

"Glad you're pleased."

"No point getting snotty with me, Mr. Fitzgerald. I know it ain't easy. But I am telling you it was right to say you'd like some time to think it over. That was using your head."

"Sorry, Windy. I guess I spoke that way because it has been a strain."

The scout smiled at the younger man, not at all ruffled by his sarcasm. "You know the Sioux, they sometimes takes three whole days to think somethin' out."

"Three days? No wonder things go so slowly with them." Fitzgerald shook his head ruefully. "By then the battle is over."

"Maybe. Maybe it's over when you don't even allow three minutes."

"But why three days?"

"On account of they know a man don't stay the

same all the time. He changes. What he agrees to today, he don't agree to tomorrow. Like that. So they let the time pass and try to figure what they *really* see about somethin'. They figure that way a man's got a better chance of keepin' his word, on account of he knows what he's sayin' and where it's comin' from."

Fitzgerald stared incredulously at the scout. "You're not suggesting that we take three days to figure out what to do?"

"Nope. Just don't be hasty, is all I am once again saying." And Windy dropped his eyelid over his right eye, as solemn as a preacher at a funeral, while the left eye stayed wide open.

Fitzgerald wanted to break out laughing, and would have done so if he hadn't been overwhelmed with the enormity of the decision he was being called upon to make.

"I just don't get it," he said after a moment. "What did he mean about Young Bear and Cricket dying as warriors attacking an enemy? I still don't understand it. And I wanted to ask him, dammit, only you insisted we leave." He frowned at the tall scout, his irritation deepening as he felt his own inadequacy.

"That would have been foolish, showing your ignorance to them like that. I pulled you out of there so's I could explain it to you private."

"I appreciate that. Really I do," Fitzgerald added quickly, for fear Windy might think he was again being sarcastic.

Windy spat a long stream of tobacco juice at some dried horse manure just in front of where they were

151

now standing. "See, the council there, they decided that Young Bear and Cricket got to die."

"But that is exactly what I was saying in the first place," Fitzgerald insisted. "Not that they had to actually die," he corrected himself quickly. "But that they had to be taken by the army to stand trial, and then, if they were found guilty, they would be hanged or shot—punished, at any rate."

"Exceptin' it ain't quite exactly the way them in there was putting it," Windy said. "See, they want them two punished. They have sentenced them to die, but like warriors, not with their hands tied behind them and a rope around their necks, and strung up with a lot of damn fools gawkin' at 'em."

"So Cut Hand wants them to attack us and we kill them. Windy, that is murder. Two men attacking a whole platoon—it's mad, crazy! It is murder!" he repeated.

"For them it's justice," Windy said. "Justice with honor."

"But if we kill those two like that, we could have a war on our hands."

"You already got a war on your hands, mister, if you *don't* do it."

Fitzgerald stared at the ground at his feet. "But I can't agree to a thing like that. I can't decide something like that!"

Windy spat the whole of his chew out of his mouth. It went flying through the air and gave a wet plopping sound as it struck the trunk of a small tree. Then he leaned slightly forward and blew his nose through his thumb and forefinger, each nostril in turn.

"Son," he said finally, "you got to."

Fitzgerald was wagging his head dolefully from side to side.

Windy made his final point. "Lieutenant, that feller Tooth—him who fixed up that soldier's hair—he had to make a decision, and he made it. There was no time to lose. And we don't have so damn much time to lose, neither. It's the Sioux way of justice. You know, the whites don't own all the justice in the world."

"But Tooth was sewing on a man's scalp. That's not the same."

"Son, I know Tooth. I know his kind, is what I mean. And you can take it from this old scout—he would've done it just the same, just as sure as if he'd been sewing on that soldier's ass."

fifteen _____

"Sweetwater! I have a strong suspicion that you have been lacing my sarsaparilla with whiskey, by damn!" roared Colonel Jonathan Blue.

"Why no, Colonel, sir. I sure wouldn't even *think* of doing such a thing." Sweetwater's eyes were big, round, and innocent. "It's just that in Smith's Town here, the sassy-sprilla has got hair on it like everythin' else."

"Includin' the girls!" chuckled a toothless old-timer, sucking on his gums as he stood beside Harold the Wizard at the dice table.

"Damn your eyes, Sweetwater!" But there was no real anger in the colonel's words, as the scout reached for the dice that Harold the Wizard had tossed him.

The frame had started with the Wizard covering a couple of large bets, losing one and winning the other. After he had passed the dice to Sweetwater, the scout came out on a five and offered to borrow on the four-three draw for five dollars.

"I always bet on the make when it's nines and fives," the Wizard said.

"I'll make it for five dollars."

"Make it ten," the Wizard said, shoving in a stack of cartwheels.

Sweetwater called almost simultaneously with the throw of the dice.

The Wizard's soft white hand flashed under the overhead lamp as, without even looking down, he reached out and caught the dice. He was wearing a diamond ring on his little finger, the soft fat piling up around it like a collar.

"Five more you don't make it," he said as he threw the dice back to Sweetwater.

Sweetwater John counted out the money and threw the dice hard against the table railing. They spun around a good bit before settling.

Sweetwater's jaw dropped open as he looked down at the four-three.

"Tough," Harold the Wizard said.

"I'd like a shot at it," Jonathan Blue suddenly said, but Sweetwater was already holding his arm and rushing him to the bar.

"You crazy, Colonel? That Wizard'll strip you down to the bare bones."

Blue was pulling at his arm, but the force of Sweetwater was too great. Together they all but crashed into the bar.

"Johnson, I lent you the money to do your gambling—of which I highly disapprove, as you know—and now I demand the right to try the game myself!"

"Listen to me, Colonel. I got to educate you some. That Harold, he switches them tops and flats like he was counting money. And nobody can see him, he is that fast."

"You mean he cheats?"

"Sure he does. But keep your voice down."

"And you keep yours down, and stop calling me 'Colonel' in this place." Blue's eyes darted about the room. "But why do you let him get away with it," he demanded, "If you know that about him, and you are sure?"

"Colonel—I mean, Mr. Blue . . ." Blue was holding his hands against his ears, grimacing. "Well, what'll I call you, then?" Sweetwater's face went blank for a moment, and then lit up. "I'll call you Custer, by God!"

Jonathan Blue beamed.

"Like I say," Sweetwater resumed, "you need to get educated. See, I only dropped a little money. Thing is, see, you let the Wizard get away with it, let him win, he feels pretty good then, feels by God he is somebody. Then he'll be a helluva lot more likely to help a feller. Like us meeting up with Poker Jake and like that. You understand?"

The colonel pouted, looking even more like a pigeon, but then the huge Stetson hat began to move. His companion accepted that slight movement as a nod of agreement.

"We'll have us another round," Sweetwater said, signaling the bartender.

"I want straight sarsaparilla this time, Johnson!"

"Custer, I'm seein' to it you stay as sober as a watched puritan. Don't give it a worry!"

"I do not approve of any of this, Johnson, as you well know—or *should,* by heaven!"

To the big bartender with the bright red suspenders, Sweetwater said, "Quince, you give Mr. Custer here whatever he needs. I mean, he wants straight sassy-sprilla." And he winked with the eye that was away from Blue. "This man wants to stay sober."

Blue turned abruptly to face the scout. "I must demand some action, Johnson. We have been here for some hours now, and you still have not produced the leader of the whiskey enterprise. I have gone along with your foolishness. I know you have been trying to feed me whiskey." He paused, squinting up at Sweetwater Johnson, who towered above him, then shook his head and continued, "You fool, Johnson. Why, in the old days I could have drunk you under the table with one hand tied behind my back. Back in Kansas—and back at the Point—I could drink any man as stiff as a post and still dance the whole night long."

Sweetwater beamed on him, breathing alcohol fumes onto the colonel's perspiring forehead. "And you could screw all night long, too, Colonel? By God, I'll bet you could! Colonel—I mean, Custer—by God, I have knowed all along you been hidin' your *true* abilities under a mess of military bullshit!"

"I have never believed in familiarity, Johnson," Blue admitted. "It does breed contempt."

Sweetwater chuckled. "Speaking of familiarity, Colonel, you recollect I told you they got some cute little morsels in them upstairs rooms, and out there dancin', too."

"You mean . . . women?"

"I ain't talkin' about hosses."

"I don't wish even to discuss or hear such outrageous talk, Johnson! You will surely end up holding a pitchfork!"

The big scout shook with laughter, almost upsetting his drink, and breathing tobacco, spittle, and garlic into his companion's face, to the latter's fury.

"Now you stop this idiotic talk!"

"Custer, sir . . ." The scout winked, and lowering his voice to a loud whisper, which only infuriated Blue the more, he said, "Just remindin' you, they got a back door goes up to the cribs upstairs. Meanin' you can get in upstairs unbeknownst to anyone in this here room." He winked, and Blue turned red with anger. "Just wanted you to know the way of it. Shit, a man's got to get his axle greased every so often, now don't he?"

Blue, turning away, attempted to lean on the bar, but this was difficult for him because of his height.

He did manage it, but he was uncomfortable, feeling lost in his buckskins, which were large for him anyway.

They continued to stand at the bar for some time, Sweetwater telling endless stories of the frontier. The colonel, unbending further, though with momentary relapses into his military and crusading stance, began to recount some of his own adventures from his early days in the army.

They stood close together, the huge scout and the short man in his still incredibly clean buckskins. Blue was still wearing his big Stetson hat, though now, after several "sassy-sprillas," it was slightly askew.

Jonathan Blue was just about to launch into a long tale of an event that had occurred while he was at Richmond after Grant had taken it, when Harold the Wizard came over to where they were standing.

"Jake is free now. She just come in." And he threw his eyes, without moving his head, in the direction of the door at the other end of the bar.

"By George!" Blue, in his enthusiasm, almost dropped his glass. "At last! We'll settle this thing now, once and for all!" He reached up and pulled his big hat further down on his head and, turning abruptly, slapped Sweetwater on the arm to follow.

But he was too fast. Perhaps the wide brim of his hat obstructed his vision, but in any case he failed to see the wide-mouthed spittoon into which he stepped firmly, causing him to fall facedown on the floor.

Somebody guffawed. The colonel tried to rise, his nose streaming blood, but his foot was locked in the cuspidor. A roar of laughter rocked the room as, cursing, Blue finally reached his feet, with Sweetwater's help. But his foot was still in the cuspidor, which he was trying in vain to shake loose.

"Colonel, you'd best sit down," Sweetwater said, shoving a chair under Blue.

"Will you stop calling me 'Colonel'!"

"Forgot."

"Damn!"

"Hold onto the seat there, an' I'll yank the sonofabitch off of your foot."

Sweetwater faced Blue and, grabbing the cuspidor, tried as hard as he could to pull it off. But it was stuck firmly.

"Try t'other way," someone said.

With his back to the colonel, Sweetwater took the spittoon between his own legs and with all his strength tried to remove it, while Blue pressed his free foot against the scout's back.

"Sweetwater, let 'er rip!" roared someone, and somebody else cut loose with a Texas yell.

Suddenly, with a screech of pain from Jonathan Blue, the cuspidor came free, sending the colonel flying over backwards in his chair, and Sweetwater, still gripping the spittoon, charging headfirst into the bar. Only the most extreme action on the part of a half-dozen terrified customers saved the bar from destruction.

Meanwhile, Jonathan Blue lay supine on the floor, holding a reeking bar rag against his bleeding nose.

Eager hands now helped the colonel to his feet. But it immediately developed that he was unable either to stand or walk on his injured foot.

"Dammit, Johnson! I have twisted and possibly broken my foot or ankle!" Wincing in pain, the colonel sank into a chair that Harold the Wizard proffered.

"Better take him upstairs," the Wizard said, "where he can lie down. Somebody get Doc to take a looksee."

It was Sweetwater John Johnson who performed yeoman's service at this point. In pain himself, as a result of smashing his head into the wooden bar, he lifted Blue heroically onto his back as though he were a child, and carried him piggyback up the stairs to the balcony overlooking the big room.

It was a tremendous moment, an event to be recounted in days and years to come. People moved inevitably to the bar, and the Wizard himself had to help Quince in dispensing refreshment. The room hummed with excitement in a dozen keys. While customers drank and exchanged eyewitness reports, the offending cuspidor remained in solitary confinement beneath the faro table, where, in the furor, it had been kicked. No one gave it a second look.

Sweetwater and his passenger reached the balcony in only a moment. The big man wasn't even puffing.

"Put him in Dolores's room," somebody said.

"No, put him in here," said a crisp feminine voice. "On the bed there. I'll take care of that foot while someone gets Doc."

Sweetwater laid Jonathan Blue carefully on the bed. "Good enough, Connie," he said, and passed his admiring eyes over the ample body of the still youthful blonde. The colonel continued to hold the filthy, whiskey-soaked rag to his nose, which was still bleeding. He had closed his eyes, however, and when the door shut behind Sweetwater and two other men who had accompanied him, he didn't move. He lay on his back on the wide brass bed, absolutely still, his eyes firmly shut.

The bedsprings twanged, and he felt the mattress give as the woman sat down on the edge of the bed.

"Bunny, they're gone now," she said. "You can open your eyes."

sixteen _____

In a small natural clearing surrounded by stunted spruce, First Platoon waited.

"No one—repeat, no one, nobody—is to fire a shot unless I give the order!" There was no equivocation in the young lieutenant as he walked the length of the formation, accompanied by Windy Mandalian and Sergeant Gus Olsen.

"You will be in skirmish position," he continued. "But only Private Fegan will fire. I want that clearly understood. I will give the order when Fegan is to fire, and where. You will hear the shots, but *you will not fire!*" He paused, standing stiffly before them, letting it sink in. "If anything should change, if anything should go in an unexpected way, you will receive orders, or you will hear the bugler. Are there any questions?"

The silence carried a great many questions, but none were spoken. Fitzgerald had his own questions too, as he nodded to Olsen and told the sergeant to form the platoon into a skirmish line.

Turning at last to Windy, he said, "I still think this whole show is crazy. But I'm going the whole hog with it."

"You done right, son, believe me," the scout said, looking back in the direction of the Sioux village. "And it was right to pick your sharpshooter for the job. It would sure be a helluva note if whoever did the shooting missed, or only wounded them."

"So now we wait?"

"Now we wait." Windy glanced at the young officer. "It will take a while. But it has to be done right."

Fitzgerald's lips were in a tight line as he spoke. "It will be done right," he said. "It will be. I gave my word to Cut Hand on that."

Now, as the scout glanced sideways at Fitzgerald, the corners of his eyes started to smile; but he didn't let it show any further. Instead, he turned it into a squint as he once again looked toward the Sioux village. Then he looked up at the sun.

"Won't be too long now," he said. And he was thinking, *Matt, you trained the young feller pretty good.*

•   •   •

In the recuperation room at Harold the Wizard's, the patient was feeling better, sufficiently better to start complaining and worrying about anyone finding out what had happened. "Anyone" meant wife, daughter, the officers and men at Stambaugh. All his life, Jonathan Blue had been exceedingly secretive about his personal life, and he was furious now that his privacy was being threatened. He lay propped on pillows in the wide bed, while his hostess straightened the covers, tucked in the sides, and made sure the covers were not too tight around the injured foot.

"Some more medicine, Bunny?"

Jonathan Blue winced, but heroically held back the reprimand that rose in him at the familiarity. "Yes, my dear. It clearly has alcohol in it, but it does mitigate the pain."

His nose had stopped bleeding, although it felt quite sore. His face was washed, thanks to his nurse, and his foot was raised slightly according to doctor's orders.

It had taken much persuasion on the part of both Connie and Sweetwater John for the colonel to accept his present condition. There wasn't anything he could do about it, anyway. Sweetwater had explained that the town's doctor was himself down with the croup, and so was unable to attend in person, but that having listened carefully to all details of the unfortunate accident, he had prescribed painkiller and rest so that removal to Fort Stambaugh and the care of an army doctor could be accomplished shortly. On reflection, the colonel saw that it made perfect sense.

Actually, it had been Clarence Lightfoot who had been consulted by Sweetwater. And Doc, with the approval of Poker Jake, had diagnosed and prescribed *in absentia*. The painkiller was, of course, Sure-Shot Panacea.

Yes, the colonel decided, it was all he could do. There wasn't anything else he could possibly do. After all, it was absolutely clear that the important thing was that nobody— absolutely no one—must hear of his presence at the Wizard's place. It had all worked beautifully, thanks to the back-door arrangement. If only he hadn't stepped into that damned spittoon! But there was nothing to be done about it now, he told himself. There was nothing he, Jonathan Blue, could do.

And yet—to his amazement—as his eyes drifted over to Connie's shapely body moving about the room, he found that he felt rotten and good at the same time. On the one hand, he was exceedingly irritated at his predicament, but on the other, his desire for the girl's youthful, willing body was more than apparent in the extraordinary rigidity of his member, which was now making a tent out of the bed covers.

And when she turned suddenly, with her lips apart, her eyes glancing wickedly at him, saying, "Bunny, what have you got there in bed with you?" he realized that the pain in his foot and the irritation over what had happened to him, with its frightful risk of discovery, were not at all the most important things on his mind. In fact, none of that was on his mind at all.

"Come here and find out for yourself, my dear," Jonathan Blue said, as he pushed back the bed covers.

• • •

At a clearing a half-mile from the Sioux camp, the waiting soldiers could hear the throbbing of drums and the chanting of the warriors.

"You know what it's about?" Fitzgerald asked as he watched the intent look on Windy Mandalian's face.

"Started with a war chant." The scout paused. "Now this here is a death song."

It was early morning, and the platoon had been in formation since before dawn, when Fitzgerald had given them their orders. But now they were at ease, waiting.

In the line there was a smattering of talk as the men coped with nervousness and boredom.

"Sounds gloomy as all hell," Malone said as the death chant continued.

"It's the death song," Stretch Dobbs said, having overheard Windy. The tallest soldier in Easy Company shifted on his big feet as the sun cleared the tops of the trees and now began to beat down on the waiting men.

"I heard one once over at Tipi Town," said Reb McBride.

"You got to be hard up, Reb, to take that blanket-Indian stuff," Malone said.

"Any port in a storm," Reb answered with a big wink. "That's where Mandalian gets all his news and gossip."

"And that's where you'll get the pox in your pecker, for Chrissakes," Malone said.

The talk moved desultorily through the ranks while the restlessness grew.

At a short distance from his companion, Pony Tom Tooth sat smoking his pipe. He had hardly spoken a word since the platoon left Outpost Number Nine, and he was now realizing how he'd sealed himself off from the others. Well, he regretted it, for he had grown fond of them. He liked them, and felt fortunate to have found such a haven, if he could call it that. Only it was something he couldn't help. The pain had suddenly become too great, and it had taken all his strength to keep from breaking down. And now, with the realization passing along the line that there might not be a fight, his wild thought of catching a bullet had gone up in smoke.

Yet he had to do something. He couldn't go on like this, day after day, night after night. He could not forget her. He didn't *want* to forget her. Only why couldn't he remember her differently? Why that terrible, endless moment of her suffering! He looked down at his hands. It could have been different. Oh, God, it could have been different!

Tooth was suddenly aware that the chanting was stronger, that it was coming closer. And as Sergeant Olsen barked a command to the platoon, he got swiftly to his feet and checked his Springfield.

"Remember—no firing," Olsen snapped as he moved swiftly along the skirmish line.

Now Tooth saw the little group of five Indians coming through the trees that bordered the Sioux camp.

The party stopped and looked at the distant line of soldiers.

"That one in the middle is Cut Hand," Malone said, his voice carrying in the still morning air.

The chief was standing very straight, as always, flanked by two older members of the tribe. To his far left were Young Bear and Cricket, in full war regalia.

Suddenly the chief moved his arm, so that the palm of his hand faced the two warriors. At the signal, they began racing toward the soldiers, their war cries piercing the clear air.

Pony Tom Tooth thought for a moment that they were coming directly at him, and he felt something clutch inside his stomach and chest.

He heard the lieutenant say something, but he couldn't tell what it was. Out of the corner of his eye, he saw Pop Fegan lift his rifle and take aim. The warrior to Tooth's left was the first to fall, as the rifle shot cracked out. The second warrior kept running, still shouting his war cry. The second shot dropped him only a few feet from his companion.

"They are deader'n hell," Malone said.

Nobody moved. A deep silence fell over the plain and the two parties that had witnessed the shooting. Cut Hand and his elders had not moved a muscle, nor had the men of First Platoon. Then Holzer coughed suddenly, and Fitzgerald gave the order to mount up.

It was as he swung into his saddle that Tooth thought he saw one of the fallen warriors move. It was the one nearest him who now raised himself on his elbow,

171

wrestling his rifle into position as the life drained from him. The platoon had turned and started to ride off as Tooth suddenly broke ranks and charged the fallen warrior.

But he had dropped his Springfield, and now, wresting his Schofield from its holster, he was already on top of the Sioux. Flinging himself out of his saddle right onto the prone warrior, he felt a tremendous blow in the chest as Cricket shot him. But he had his Scoff out now, and he shot the Indian between the eyes.

Olsen and Malone reached them first. There was no question that all three—Young Bear, Cricket, and Pony Tom Tooth—were dead.

seventeen ⸻⸻

In the upstairs quarters of Colonel Jonathan Blue, at Harold the Wizard's Good Times Parlor, "Mr. Custer" was feeling not the slightest pain in his foot or his ankle, or indeed anywhere else—not even in his conscience.

It was a most delightful convalescence, he reflected as he lay limp in the incredible satifaction of ecstasy shared with a member of the opposite sex. Connie lay exhausted on top of him. The covers had been thrown to the floor, and their naked bodies were still entwined in the softening light that came through the window as the day began slowly to die.

Neither of them heard the knock at the door. Neither of them heard the door open.

Only when someone said, "Oh, excuse me!" did the lovers, shocked into mobility, become aware that the door had not been locked. And it was as the girl rolled away from him that Jonathan Blue, as naked as Adam, lifting his head and staring bleary-eyed at his visitor, realized that his whole plan of eliminating the whiskey trains had been shot to pieces.

"Excuse me, sir. I'd received news that you'd had a serious accident, so I hurried here as quickly as I could."

At which point Matt Kincaid stepped farther into the room so that the person standing behind him could enter.

"You wanted to speak with me, Colonel?" And Poker Jake, having removed her cigar to say those words, returned it slowly to her mouth, her cold eyes surveying with total calm the naked man lying on the bed.

"Dismiss the company, Sergeant," Warner Conway said, and turned toward the bony man standing beside him in civilian clothing.

Ben Cohen's earsplitting dismissal broke across the parade, and the men began to melt back to their afternoon details.

"Well, Mr. Hounds, did you see your man?" Conway asked.

Detective Inspector Wayne Hounds of Sacramento, California, shook his long head, sniffed and scratched behind his ear, as he walked with Conway and Matt

Kincaid toward Easy Company's orderly room.

"I thank you, Captain, and Lieutenant," he said wearily. He was grayheaded and lanky, and he wore a star on his frock coat lapel and a big Navy Colt holstered at his right hip.

"Come in a minute before you take off, Mr. Hounds."

Seated in a chair in Conway's office, Hounds accepted a cigar, which he slipped into his vest pocket.

With his eyes directly on Conway, he said, "Wonder if you'd mind me talking to your first sergeant, Captain. You know, it was a real hot trail I was working on. I just can't believe that Gatty up and vanished!"

"Matt, would you ask Sergeant Cohen to come in here?" Conway said.

"Yes, sir."

"Sorry to trouble you so much, Captain Conway, but it's been a long haul and I do hate to go home empty-handed."

"I understand, Mr. Hounds. We are at your service."

"I do appreciate your cooperation, Captain."

When Kincaid came back with Ben Cohen, Conway said, "I believe you've met Sergeant Cohen. You can ask him anything you like, pertaining to the man you're looking for."

Hounds didn't waste any time, but got right down to it.

"The name's Gatty. Patrick Gatty. Supposed to have enlisted in the mounted infantry and been assigned to duty around this part of the Wyoming Territory."

Ben Cohen was already shaking his head. "Never heard of anyone with that name, Mr. Hounds."

"Could be he was using another name. Short feller, weighed about a hundred and twenty-five pounds. There was talk he'd rode for the Pony Express, though that'd have to be a lot of years back. Blue eyes. Studied medicine." The policeman's voice was deep, and at the same time had a stringy sound to it, as though he was suffering from some rheumy ailment.

"Doesn't ring anything with me," Cohen said.

"But you have had new recruits coming in."

"We always have new recruits coming in."

"This one wouldn't be young. He'd be gettin' on. Probably lied about his age."

"Sure wish I could help, sir. Try Regiment?"

"It was Regiment sent me here."

"Could I ask what you're wantin' this feller for, or is that out of line, sir?" Ben asked.

"He is wanted for killing his girlfriend."

"I see," Cohen said.

"She was pregnant. The doc said she'd die if she gave birth, so this feller Gatty—he was a medical student, he operated on her. It seems he couldn't get a regular doctor to do it, so he done it himself."

"And the girl died."

"The girl died. And Gatty, or whatever he is calling himself, is charged with killing her. I got the warrant."

Matt Kincaid leaned forward in his chair now. "Mr. Hounds, I know nothing about these things, but doesn't the fact that he was trying to save her life make any difference?"

"Not with her maw and paw." Hounds paused, his deep eyes feeling suspiciously over Matt's face. "I know what you're sayin', Lieutenant, and more'n likely nothin' would happen to him. I mean, he *was* tryin' to save her life. I do agree. But her folks are—well, they're her folks, and her paw's a power in the community, and they want him brought in to stand trial."

Conway stood up at that point, and held out his hand. "If we hear anything that might be of help to you, Mr. Hounds, we'll let you know. Meanwhile, I'm sorry you've wasted a long trip out here."

Hounds looked around at all three men in the room, and Kincaid thought, *He doesn't believe us for a minute. Damn lucky the man's out of his jurisdiction, and the army's not obligated to help him in any case.*

It was obvious even to Hounds that Kincaid's thought was shared by the other two soldiers in the room, but the man from Sacramento knew there wasn't a damn thing he could do about it. He nodded at the three men, placed his Stetson on his head, and walked out to the parade and his waiting horse.

When Windy Mandalian walked in five minutes later, Conway was lighting a cigar.

"Looks like we had that funeral for Tooth just in time, Captain."

Conway sighed, releasing a little cloud of cigar smoke as he did so. "You are so right."

"He is Gatty, isn't he?"

"He has got to be," Matt said. "A hundred and twenty-five pounds, used to ride for the Pony Express,

177

blue eyes, and studied medicine."

"If I was writing a story for an Eastern newspaper, I'd bet on Tooth being Gatty," Conway said. "But as a CO in Wyoming Territory, the only Tooth I know is a man who acted with heroism not once, but twice." He looked over at Kincaid, who was nodding his head.

"I concur with that completely, sir."

Conway laid his cigar down in the ashtray at his elbow. "And if it hadn't been for our ingenious adjutant, who knows where we'd be getting our next drink of liquor from—if at all!" And he reached into the desk drawer and brought out a bottle of brandy and three glasses.

In silence the captain poured, then raised his glass in a silent toast. The three men took the brandy in a single swallow.

"Matt, I don't know how you did it. I think it's better that I don't know. But there's no question, Colonel Blue is laying off the whiskey trains. The boys—whipsawed by Poker Jake—will continue bringing whiskey through Muddy Gap and Whisper Creek as before. Cut Hand is happy, because Jake is making sure the Indians don't get any firewater from Otis Birdwhistle. Otis, it seems, has decided suddenly to leave the country. All is well."

"Sir, just one thing," Matt said. "I'd like it to be known for the record that it was not I who engineered this happy conclusion, but one Sweetwater John Johnson."

Conway grinned. "I'll take your word for that, Lieutenant." And he reached for the bottle of brandy. "If not with a dose of salt, for certain with a stiff shot of brandy."

There was a knock at the door, and Ben Cohen entered.

"Captain, Tooth's belongings are out in the orderly room, as you suggested, since there's no family. And I've let the men know that if there is anything of his they might want—as a memento—they could ask for it. Would you care to see what there is, sir?"

When Conway, Kincaid, and Windy Mandalian went out to the orderly room, they found about a dozen men from First Platoon standing there. Tooth's belongings were spread on the first sergeant's desk.

"If there is something any of you would want of Tooth's, you may ask for it," Conway said. "There's no family we can send anything to. I know he had good friends in the company." He paused. "So take a look."

It didn't take long; Tooth's possessions were few. Besides his toilet articles, there were two books, his pipe and a half-empty pouch of tobacco, a civilian shirt, and his wallet, which was empty. It had been decided to put his last pay into the enlisted men's fund.

"I'd like that shirt," Reb McBride said.

Cohen nodded. "Take it, then, unless someone else wants it."

"And I'd like one of those books," Malone said. "Won't hurt to read something, maybe."

"I'll take the other book," Dobbs said.

Wolfgang Holzer pointed at Tooth's pipe. Ben Cohen handed him the pipe and the tobacco pouch.

"That leaves his toilet articles. Hell, you've all got that stuff," Cohen said, and started picking up the razor, the shaving brush, and the comb.

At that moment, Coy Flanagan stepped forward and pointed. "Could I have that, Sarge?"

Ben Cohen looked at Coy Flanagan's bright red thatch of hair. Then he looked down at where Flanagan was pointing. "Yeah," he said. "Sure. I bet Tooth would like you to have his comb."